JAP

A TEMPORARY LOVER

Sophie Shaw had taken pride and pleasure in building up a veterinary practice with her husband Michael and his partner, but Michael's death had left a void in her life. It seemed none of the applicants for the practice was right — until Luke Jordon pointed out that *she* was the problem. Once Luke began his duties, Sophie had to admit that he was an excellent vet, but he also raised a frisson in her that had nothing to do with work . . .

CAROL WOOD

A TEMPORARY LOVER

Complete and Unabridged

LINFORD
Leicester

First published in Great Britain in 1995

First Linford Edition
published 2014

A catalogue record for this book is available
from the British Library.

ISBN 978–1–4448–1903–8

Published by
F. A. Thorpe (Publishing)
Anstey, Leicestershire

Set by Words & Graphics Ltd.
Anstey, Leicestershire
Printed and bound in Great Britain by
T. J. International Ltd., Padstow, Cornwall

This book is printed on acid-free paper

1

A mellow spring breeze gently skimmed the tops of the Kent fields running north of Cranthorpe.

Sophie gazed from the bedroom window, her golden-brown eyes dazzled by the intensity of colour and scale of the landscape. The raw sienna bricks of the funnels towering above the converted oast houses of the adjacent practice blazed against the blue of the sky and the curving buildings under the turrets, four in all, glistened creamily in the April sunshine.

From one of the windows she saw movement. Howard would be roughly halfway through the interview. What was Luke Jordon like? she wondered anxiously, dearly wishing she could avoid finding out.

Turning a wisp of strawberry-blonde hair behind her ear and glancing one more time at her reflection, navy blue linen suit clinging to her slender five-foot-six-inch frame, she took a deep breath and left the house, calling Steamer to heel.

Fifty yards along the lane, she unlocked the five-bar gate to the practice and Steamer, his thick black Labrador tail beating furiously, pushed open the surgery door with his nose.

When Sophie thought about it later, she recalled the breath had left her body the moment she and Luke Jordon had locked eyes.

'Sophie . . . ah, good!' Howard, the senior partner of the practice, exclaimed as she tried to regain her breath. 'Just the person we were talking about. In fact, we were coming across to the house to find you. I've just given Luke the grand tour of the surgery.'

The tall black-haired man seemed to fill up the small room. Smokey blue eyes danced under their heavy lids as he held out his hand. 'I'm delighted to meet you, Mrs Shaw. May I call you Sophie?'

Her fingers engaged the firm, muscular grasp. 'I must apologise for being late . . . ' she evaded, trying not to make eye contact.

'No apologies necessary.' His gaze found its way over her with undisguised pleasure as he murmured silkily, 'Howard has been the perfect host.'

She glanced at the older man. The thatch of grey hair, which crowned a deceptively agile physique for a man of fifty-five, was ruffled, indicating his rushed departure from home.

Howard Oliver predictably checked his watch. 'Listen, you two . . . would you mind terribly if I ducked out for a bit? I've a pregnant mare to see and Molly would like me home for a Sunday roast for a change.'

Luke Jordon shrugged broad shoulders under a perfectly tailored sports jacket. 'Of course. I'm sorry I had to disturb your Sunday, but it was the only time I had free. Thanks for all your help this afternoon. I'm sure Sophie and I will get along just fine.' He turned the almost luminous blue eyes in her direction, together with a smile that produced a stunning set of even white teeth, and Sophie found herself mesmerised.

'Er — I'll just walk you to the car, Howard,' she suggested quickly, feeling decidedly in need of a breath of fresh air. 'Meanwhile, no doubt Mr Jordon can find his way around for a second look.'

The senior partner raised his hand in farewell. 'Luke, I hope we'll see you again very soon.'

They walked into the bright afternoon, following the narrow path around to the car park well hidden behind the clusters of thick green privet. 'I like him, Sophie,' Howard told her cheerfully. 'He's a damn good vet, knows a thing or two about new techniques — been abroad with all the top people. Just the kind of new blood we need.'

At her reluctance to enthuse, Howard

sighed. 'Sophie, we have to have a partner. We can't go on like this. Greg Barton has held off leaving for as long as he can. The equine vet in the north will only temporarily hold open his job.'

Knowing full well Greg Barton had his heart set on becoming an equine specialist made it no easier for Sophie to agree. Nor did the fact that John Marks, barely out of his second fully qualified year, could hardly be expected to shoulder the extra work. But Howard's health worried her most as the only senior partner left after her husband's death. Under the pressure he was wretchedly exhausted.

'It's two years since Michael died,' Howard reminded her gently. 'And it's about time you started to live again. A healthy young woman of twenty-eight can't simply live for her work — '

'I know.' Sophie lifted her small shoulders. 'But replacing Michael is so . . . difficult.'

The older man nodded, sighed

deeply and slumped into the driving seat. 'I'm sorry, Sophie, I don't want to upset you, but we'll soon be down to just John and me. I can't hold the fort for much longer. I've only a few years left before I officially retire and I'd like to see the practice well on its feet by then — for your sake apart from my own peace of mind.'

They must come to some decision, she knew. They had seen more than enough unsuitable candidates. It was up to her, as practice manager, with all her and Michael's hard work and savings invested in the business, to make certain the practice flourished, and that meant a full team.

'I'll talk to him,' she compromised, smiling weakly.

'Good girl. I'll bet you this one's right for the practice!'

In silence she stared up at the conicals, symbols of the practice she and Michael had birthed. Sometimes all their work seemed in vain . . .

'Having second thoughts?' Luke

Jordon made her jump as he appeared beside her.

'Second thoughts?' she repeated, frowning. 'On what?'

'Why, me, of course. It's a big decision taking someone into the fold. And it must be more so, in your case.'

'My case?' she asked again stupidly.

'Howard told me what a rough time you've had. To try looking for someone to match up to your husband — '

'No one could 'match up' to him, Mr Jordon,' she cut in icily. 'I'm not looking for a replacement for Michael in any sense of the word.'

He quirked a dark eyebrow. 'Aren't you? Correct me if I'm wrong, but I appear to be the most recent of a long line of candidates, all of whom you've turned down.'

'Because they weren't what we wanted.'

'Weren't what *you* wanted,' he stressed bluntly.

'Did Howard tell you that?'

'Didn't need to.' He gave her a wry

7

smile. 'I know enough about women to recognise a brick wall before I run into it.'

Sophie raised her eyebrows. 'I'm sure your knowledge of women is extensive. However, there's no brick wall — as you put it.'

'Glad to hear I was wrong.' He gave another spectacular grin as he took her elbow and moved her along the path. 'Now, I wonder, if I promise to behave myself, could we see the practice again, together?'

'We seem to be heading in that direction anyway,' Sophie mumbled as he steered her past the hedge. Even Steamer seemed to be won over, happy to trot alongside the well-heeled shoes. As she glanced under her lashes at him she also had the disconcerting sensation he seemed to be enjoying her discomfort. Well, at least he'd admitted to being a rampant flirt — not at all the sort of man she had in mind for the practice, but then, she knew in her heart there would never be anyone like Michael.

Ten minutes later Sophie stood in the admissions-room, repeating her carefully worded speech, the one she had made at least five or six times to interested parties. 'The nurse flashes the patient's details up onto the video screen,' she patiently explained, somewhat put off by the long, muscular legs ambling around the room, 'and the client signs the consent forms. Our nurse briefly examines the patient, checks for problems, then gives the pre-med and — '

'A bit like painting by numbers.'

'I'm sorry?' Sophie's mouth fell open.

'Everything's perfect,' he shrugged. 'Does anything ever go wrong? I mean, like painting blue where red should be?'

She sighed, folding her arms, resisting his teasing smile. 'I'm not sure that's a particularly accurate metaphor. I think perhaps before we get too bogged down with detail we'd better see the dispensary and laboratory.'

'Nothing like a bit of colour in life,' she heard him remark breezily as she walked ahead, and, smothering a grin, she couldn't help silently agreeing.

For colour, she decided, had been missing in her life for what seemed an eternity. Her brain had been so attuned to work sometimes she felt she'd lost the ability to see anything else other than black and white and a few depressing greys. Now she did laugh quietly to herself as she decided Luke Jordon's metaphor disease was spreading rapidly!

'You look beautiful when you smile.'

She hadn't realised, but he'd been watching her, and her embarrassment wasn't helped by his evident and wholehearted enjoyment of it — or by the fact she had been told she looked beautiful, and, though probably quite untrue, it was, all the same, very flattering. She laughed again despite herself.

'That's better,' he chuckled, 'much, much better.'

She decided to let him win that one. 'I told Howard he sounded like a politician — but you leave him standing.'

He made a slow, exaggerated bow. 'Why, thank you. I take it that's a compliment?'

'Take it whichever way you like, but I really think we should progress, Mr — '

'Luke,' His full lips pushed out. 'Try it. The name's ridiculously easy once you get the hang of it.'

'Luke,' she mumbled reluctantly, her cheeks flushing. She took a steadying breath. 'In this room we print our own labels on the computer, applying standard warnings and instructions. The nurses do all the blood testing in the lab, keeping the vaccines in the cold-drinks fridge — '

'You enjoy your work as practice manager?' he cut in once more.

'Why?' she asked, exasperated at having to stop again.

'I just wondered. You don't really look the figures type.' His eyes

11

descended over her slim figure and predictably he added, 'Except for the perfect one I see standing here before me, of course.'

She made no attempt to argue. 'If you must know, I'm a VN, basically. But since we married we became so busy I took on the administration side. Now, is there anything else you would like to know — Luke?'

'Yes. Will you have dinner with me this evening?'

'Why should I do that?' she asked uncertainly.

'Because I want to know more about the practice.'

She paused. 'With a view to a partnership?'

He nodded. 'With a view to a partnership.'

She gave a small sigh. Now she was trapped by her own words. He was genuinely interested, though heaven knew why. He just didn't seem like the type for a rural practice. But she couldn't lose much, save a little pride perhaps, and she certainly didn't think he would take no for an answer anyway.

'Is that a yes?'

She grinned. 'It's a yes. But you'd better come and see the rest of the place.'

Giving him a whirlwind tour of the consulting-rooms, the two theatres and the side-rooms used for laundry and autoclaves, they finally arrived back in Reception.

'It's all pretty stunning.' He frowned up at the conicals above. 'You've left it all in character, but it's modern and well equipped; you must be very proud of yourselves.'

Sophie nodded. 'It took a long while, lots of hard work and still is, really.'

He shot her an odd look. 'Don't you ever have time for fun?'

'It depends on what you mean by fun.' She avoided his gaze. 'You don't put years of hard work at risk by leaving it all to luck. Now, what time this evening?'

'Eight suit you?'

'Fine. Where shall I meet you?' she asked quickly.

He frowned. 'No way. I'll pick you up. I'm an old-fashioned guy at heart and, besides, you'll want to drink champagne.'

She laughed. 'I will? Any special reason?'

'Our long and lasting partnership, of course.'

Her smile faded. 'Luke, this is a preliminary discussion. Don't take anything for granted.'

He raised innocent blue eyes. 'As if I would.' Shamelessly allowing his gaze to linger on her mouth, he said in slow, husky tones that sent a chill down her spine, 'I like what I see, Sophie — very much. You won't find me a difficult man to handle.'

★   ★   ★

A remark Sophie seriously doubted as she sipped at the sparkling Krug champagne later that evening, wondering how on earth she had let herself be persuaded into a premature celebration. Wondering, too, why she had bothered so much with her appearance, having decided to wear a stunning black dress. With its simple cut, it enhanced the swell of her full, feminine breasts and had drawn instant appraisal from Luke's blue eyes the minute they had landed on her.

Luke himself had been impressive in casual clothes during the afternoon but in a crisp black dinner suit he looked devastating. Treated to the sight of his broad shoulders and long legs virtually blocking the light from her doorway, she had managed to regain her composure as they sped into the country in his comfortable bottle-green Jaguar.

Journey and arrival at the country inn successfully accomplished, Sophie nibbled at her fresh trout.

'What makes you want the Oliver Shaw practice so much?' she asked, unable to match the healthy appetite opposite her.

'It feels right.' He licked his moist lips. 'Gut instinct, perhaps.'

Sophie smiled ruefully. 'Do you always go by gut instinct?'

'Always.'

She hesitated. 'The investment will be considerable . . . '

He shrugged carelessly, wiping his mouth with a napkin, flicking his eyes up to meet hers. 'If you're anxious, I can have the money tied up within the week.'

She mumbled something noncommittal, remembering Howard had told her that Luke Jordon had posed no concern as far as financial reliability went.

He looked at her curiously. 'Tell me about Michael,' he prompted.

'There's no point,' she answered coolly. 'We came to talk about the practice.'

He shrugged. 'Then tell me about your father-in-law. He began the

16

conversion of the oast houses, didn't he?'

Sophie paused. 'The original practice was in Cranthorpe. The oast houses and the grain stores which are now the VN's accommodation, came on the market when Michael was taking his finals. Dick Shaw thought the property would make an ideal investment for the future. It was always understood Michael would come in as junior partner.'

The blue eyes widened fractionally. 'Then you married?'

'I was twenty, Michael five years older. He was my brother's friend at school.'

'Were you and Michael happy?'

She stiffened. 'That isn't relevant.'

'Coward.'

'We were very happy,' she was quick to assure him. 'We had a good marriage and a wonderful working relationship.'

He sat back in his chair, one eyebrow raised. 'A marriage made in heaven?'

'If you like, yes.'

17

He shrugged. 'Not many of those about these days. A perfect marriage is a kind of myth, I would have said.'

'Then you haven't been in love,' she said as she looked into his eyes.

He nodded slowly. 'Obviously not. I wonder — '

'Let's talk about the practice,' she diverted firmly. 'You're quite serious about the partnership?'

He grinned. 'Absolutely.'

'Then I suggest a three-month trial period so that everyone has time to find out how they work together.'

He nodded. 'Fine by me.' He picked up his glass and held it in the air. 'To us.'

Sophie's face fell. 'You've no objections . . . stipulations . . . demands of your own?'

'I told you, I'm not a difficult man to handle.' He gestured to the delicious sweet of iced meringue set before them. 'Now, can we relax a little?'

She took a breath, her eyes avoiding him, and, pretending to concentrate on the frothy meringue, smothered her thudding heart with gulps of cold icecream. She told herself at least she had the guarantee of the three-month trial period behind her and, at worst, when it didn't work out — as she was sure it wouldn't — they could advertise again after the summer.

'Wouldn't you like to know something about me?' he asked softly, making her jerk up her head. 'Don't I inspire the least little bit of curiosity?'

Her brown eyes sparkled. 'I was sure you would get around to telling me.'

He chuckled. 'Ouch!'

She raised an eyebrow. 'You're aching to tell me, aren't you?'

'Only if you insist.' He lifted his blue eyes thoughtfully, considering the ceiling for inspiration. 'OK, let me see. I was born in Kent. My sister Louise and I boarded after our parents' marriage broke up when I was ten and Louise eight. I decided I wanted to be a vet because my father was a barrister and I detested the thought of all those gowns and wigs and long speeches. At the time becoming a vet seemed a rebellious enough thing to do, but I was lucky in so far as I took to training like a duck to water — forgive the pun again.' He grinned at her suppressed laughter. 'Are you still awake? Shall I continue? Riveting stuff, isn't it?' he asked her with teasing eyes.

She couldn't help smiling, admiring the easy self-mockery, knowing he had deliberately glossed over what she suspected was a difficult upbringing. Divorce and boarding-school, separation from his parents and his sister. For all his apparent ease, he must have fought to survive an unhappy childhood.

'Your parents are alive?' she asked, curious now.

'My father died while I was working in Canada last year with a group of vets in Ontario. My mother remarried and lives in Scotland. We don't get to see each other much. She has a busy life in charity work.' He shrugged. 'Louise I see more often.' His eyes softened as he talked of his sister. 'Her husband Martin is a nice guy, a teacher. And Pip, their eight-year-old minx of a daughter, is a holy terror. Louise is a good mum. Happy families again.'

'Cynic,' she threw at him.

'Maybe. I'm afraid I probably am.'

'And you've never married?'

He grinned. 'I've now reached thirty-three and I have to say I don't believe in myths.'

'You are a cynic.'

'And you look a very sexy lady in that lovely dress.'

Sophie blushed. 'You're changing the subject.'

'Deliberately,' he assured her with a rueful smile. 'Sophie, I have to tell you this — I'm not a time-waster,' he murmured. 'I know what I want. I've always known what I wanted. And I want the practice.'

The laughter died from her lips. 'A partnership in the practice,' she corrected him quickly.

21

'A partnership. The same thing.'

'I shall of course have to speak to Howard — '

'Howard agrees,' he cut in smoothly. 'When we talked he gave me every indication he was satisfied.'

She studied him carefully, the intense blue eyes which were masked by lazy amusement held at their centre a determined spark of ambition. An easy man to handle, he said. She wondered again how misleading this statement might prove to be. 'You're very sure of yourself,' she said softly.

'I make it my job to be. As for the legal side of things . . . we'll let the solicitors earn their money. Now, how about some coffee?'

Sophie realised she hadn't stood a chance from the very beginning. He'd had it all planned. Well, what did it matter? What was the point of resisting at this juncture? He could have his way for the moment, for three months. Then, if she wasn't happy she could terminate any future dealings with

Luke Jordon. She would make sure their contracts contained a mutual termination clause specifically for that purpose.

Pushing all her doubts to the back of her mind, she smiled and raised her glass.

★   ★   ★

Two weeks later Sophie smoothed down the elegant cream summerweight suit hugging her feminine figure. Her gaze was directed at the bungalow where Luke had temporarily taken up residence with its pocket-sized lawn and showering of summer flowers.

'I'm looking for a house in Cranthorpe,' he'd told them, even though she had pointed out that things might not work to their mutual satisfaction. He had just given them a charmed smile. 'No problem,' he'd shrugged.

With his presence so close, Sophie found her attention distracted and this, their first working morning, was a test of her nerves as she sat at her desk in the office.

Lucy, the dark-haired young nurse, had worked at the practice for three years and supervised the two younger nurses who lived in. Now she frowned at Sophie as they checked the written schedules.

'Luke will be in consulting-room one, John is remaining in the locum's room and Howard of course is in his own as usual,' she murmured, following the tip of her pencil as she sketched in the rota.

Sophie nodded with a sigh. 'All systems go.'

'Luke's nice. I think he'll fit in well here,' Lucy said, her cheeks growing red as she buried her head in her writing.

Sophie grinned, despite her anxiety that Luke would prove an unabashed flirt with the staff. Perhaps a little colour was what the practice needed anyway, as Luke himself had so helpfully pointed out.

For two years the practice had been

in the doldrums. Shock waves had rippled for months after Michael's accident. The suddenness of it was the most unacceptable, his car running off the road in icy weather and pitch blackness. It had ended up an unrecognisable tangle.

Michael. The love of her life. He'd been her first boyfriend, the only man she'd ever made love with. As she thought of him a hand gripped her heart and twisted it as she tried to bury the grief. If only they had had a child.

Sophie thrust the unhappy memories from her mind, dragging her attention back to the waiting nurse. 'How many admissions this morning, Lucy?'

'Six so far. Luke is taking open surgery and Howard is in theatre. John is on appointments and standby for emergencies. We've no farm calls until later.'

Sophie nodded, satisfied. 'I've a lot of paperwork to get through here. Will you girls be able to cope?'

Lucy glanced at her watch. 'Imelda is

25

here and Jane comes in this afternoon. I'll assist Howard when he needs me . . . yes, for a Monday — '

'Lucy!' Imelda's summons drew Lucy's eyes upward.

'I spoke too soon,' she sighed, turning on her heel, followed closely by Sophie.

In Reception they found Luke and the trainee, Imelda, crouching over a dog. 'Heart attack,' Luke said quietly as Sophie knelt beside him. 'Let's get him into my room.'

Leaving the girls and Luke to lift the Great Dane onto the animal stretcher, Sophie hurried along to his consulting-room. She swiftly prepared a syringe with a heart-stimulant drug and as they laid the stretcher on the examination bench, she turned to hand it to Luke.

His eyes lifted gratefully. 'Thanks. Can someone see to the owner?'

Sophie organised Imelda in the direction of a sobbing woman standing in the corridor, telling her to make her a strong, hot drink in the office, where she could sit quietly.

Returning to help Luke, she noted the dog's abdomen was enlarged with fluid.

'He must have been unwell long before he came to us,' she frowned anxiously. 'Plus he's nine, so the owner says. I've a feeling I remember seeing him once before . . .'

Luke was about to speak when the dog's eyelids quivered and a front paw jerked. He found a pulse and a small, relieved smile edged his mouth. 'Phew! That was a close call.'

Sophie felt the tension ease from her shoulders. 'Too close. More stimulant, do you think?'

'Let's wait and see. This has probably done the trick. What's his name?'

'Siegfried,' she smiled and saw him bend to lift the silky flap of ear and whisper into it. Finally Siegfried blinked his great brown eyes, his soft tongue coming out to lick Luke's cheek.

'Good chap,' he grinned, fondling the old, tired head.

As he moved, Sophie felt his arm touch hers. She could also feel his body heat doing incredible things to her pulse-rate.

'Too close for comfort?' he whispered appropriately as she took a breath at the electricity zipping between them.

2

Fifteen minutes later, when Siegfried the Great Dane rested on the floor beside his owner, Sophie told herself it was simply being back in the nursing mode which had caused the phenomenon between her and Luke. She hadn't assisted anyone in a clinical sense since Michael's death. For a few seconds everything had flooded back. This consulting-room had been Michael's — suddenly, time had stood still.

The client, recovered, bent to put on the dog's lead. 'I'll take him home now,' she said, trying to pull him up.

Luke glanced at Sophie. 'I don't think that's a particularly good idea, Mrs Farley.'

The woman frowned, staring up at them. 'Why? He looks fine to me now.'

'He may look it, but he's far from well. I'd like to do several more tests,

29

including an ultrasound, which will tell me about the chambers of his heart and what's wrong with them. When I know I'll be able to prescribe the correct medication.'

'But he doesn't need drugs. He's over his attack,' the woman protested stubbornly.

'The attack was the result of heart disease,' Luke explained patiently. 'You must have noticed Siegfried has outward signs . . . for instance, a build-up of fluid in the abdomen, breathlessness, a disinclination to move?' At her refusal to agree, Luke added, 'I also picked up a pulse deficit which indicates an abnormality, plus he has some pulmonary congestion; all this added together leads me to think he might have an enlarged heart . . . at the very least.'

'What's that in layman's terms?' the woman demanded brusquely.

'Cardiomyopathy is a chronic disorder affecting the muscle of the heart, a condition which is common in large breeds.' Luke nodded at Siegfried. 'And he's not getting any younger, is he?'

'And you're not the man I saw last time I came,' she muttered disconsolately. 'He didn't make all this fuss.'

'Then Siegfried is a patient of ours, Mrs Farley?' Sophie interrupted, reaching to flick up the details on the room's computer. She studied the screen carefully. 'Yes, you saw my husband two and a half years ago according to this. Siegfried was due to come in for more tests, but he failed to arrive.'

'Well, it just shows he didn't need tests,' Mrs Farley objected swiftly. 'I only brought him in today because he keeps refusing to budge. My husband says all he really needs is a herbal tonic.'

'If you take Siegfried away,' Luke warned in a firm voice, 'it's at your own risk — and against my advice. I shall have Mrs Shaw enter that on Siegfried's notes.'

The woman gave Luke a look to kill, Sophie noticed. 'Well, I don't seem to have much choice, do I? But my husband won't like it. He can't abide vets or doctors.'

'I'm sorry to hear it.' Luke walked to the door and opened it. 'It's entirely up to you, Mrs Farley.'

'You'll let me know when I can pick him up?'

'I'll ring,' Sophie said and checked the details of address and phone number, finally glancing at Luke as the woman hurried off.

'Michael indicated they didn't return for a follow-up check,' she sighed uneasily. 'I think it may have something to do with the husband, who I do seem to remember vaguely as not being a very co-operative man. I've a suspicion he thought there was nothing a brisk walk and fresh air wouldn't cure.'

Luke lifted his broad shoulders and sighed. 'Well, we'll just have to see how we go. Maybe if he comes in I can talk some sense into him.'

Sophie was about to say she very much doubted it, when Imelda poked her head around the door. 'Shall I take Siegfried to Recovery?'

Sophie noted how pale the girl looked. 'Imelda, are you feeling OK?' she asked in concern.

The young trainee nodded. 'It was a bit of a shock. I'd only that minute opened up and he walked in and keeled over, poor thing.'

'Stunned by those big brown eyes of yours, I expect,' Luke teased, making light of it. 'You did very well; good girl.' He handed her the lead and Sophie watched her melt under the ingenuous charm, before she finally managed to persuade Siegfried to go with her.

'No need for you to complete the paperwork,' Sophie told him briskly, tearing off the machine's print-out. 'I'll enter Siegfried's details, or at least what we know up to this moment. Now, I must get back to work.'

He pushed the door open for her and moved out of her way as she sped past. 'Research into stress-related illnesses,' he called as he followed her, 'shows that people who develop a more relaxed attitude to life live longer. A person who is always pressing ahead to the next objective and doesn't listen to that little inner voice telling them to slow down is at greater risk of heart disease — '

She swivelled around, glaring at him. 'Thank you for the advice, Dr Jordon.'

He shrugged. 'Not at all, Mrs Shaw.'

She marched off, ignoring the smile that lifted his lips. Despite this, he followed her to the office, whereupon he perched a long, well-muscled thigh on the corner of her desk as she squeezed in behind it.

She sat down with a sigh, tempted to point out that heart disease would catch up with her only after the bailiffs, who would be knocking at the door demanding payment if their invoices were not attended to promptly. Opening her mouth, she saw that it would be wasted breath. 'How can I help you?' she asked instead.

He lifted both arms. 'You already did. You quite took the wind from my sails this morning.'

'No metaphors — please, Luke, not

this morning,' she begged, sinking her elbows into the paperwork in front of her, cupping her chin in her hands.

'OK,' he agreed soberly. 'Actually I'm making a kind of apology.'

'That'll be the day.'

'Now who's the cynic?'

'Why the apology?' she persisted.

'Well, for starters — Siegfried.' He picked up a large wad of papers and flicked through it distractedly. 'You see, I thought you might just be . . . decoration, a pretty PR parcel all tied up with fancy gift-wrap. That as far as animals were concerned . . . '

Her jaw dropped. 'Well, thank you for the vote of confidence.'

He shrugged. 'I am being honest. You see, you looked too good, too delectable, to be able to do everything you said you could — plus nurse. It took a bit of stretching of the imagination — until this morning, when I didn't have to stretch it at all. You were with me every inch of the way, from the preparation of the heart stimulant right

35

down to turning up the info on the Farleys just when we needed it. You were, in a word, brilliant.'

Sophie flushed, grabbing back her file before he shredded it to pieces. 'Apology accepted,' she muttered crossly.

'Now I've offended you.' He looked at her balefully. 'You know, when Howard first interviewed me and you didn't show up for the grand tour I thought, Great, can't even be bothered to turn up for the first meeting — typical scatty woman.'

'I'm not scatty,' she reminded him dourly. 'I may be blonde but I'm not a brainless bimbo.'

He met her eyes for a long time. 'So I discovered. Apology accepted?'

She shrugged. 'I suppose so.'

He grinned. 'Well, I'd better get down to some work too.'

'If you can spare the time,' she mumbled.

'Talking of which, will you eat supper with me one evening?'

'No,' she answered flatly. 'No. No. No.'

'You're cruel.'

'Possibly. And I'm also busy.'

He stabbed a long brown finger at her paperwork. 'Remember what I told you about stress-related illness.'

She nodded. 'I remember every word . . . but at this particular moment I'm under a particularly intense form of stress called timewasting. And it has lethal repercussions!'

He threw back his head and laughed. Then to her amazement he leaned across the desk and bent to kiss the top of her head. 'You can't blame a man for trying,' he whispered huskily.

Watching him walk away, she was reminded of a recalcitrant schoolboy, shoulders drooped, legs long and loping. He looked back to give her a broad grin. 'Your hair smells lovely, by the way, like almonds.'

She watched the door close, a shiver going through her. She closed her eyes, denying the sensations that had caused her to tremble as his lips had brushed her hair. 'What's happening to me?' she croaked, swallowing hard.

The coffee percolater held a sudden attraction. She hurriedly poured a drink, allowing it to slip warmly down the back of her throat, waiting for its anaesthetic effect to calm her heart and for her upside-down world to reorganise itself back on a more familiar axis.

★　★　★

She could, Sophie thought more calmly that night as she soaked in a scented bath, ignore the whole incident or make a mountain out of a molehill. Common sense told her the new practice partner was enjoying the technical exercise. He probably asserted himself this way with most women — why should she be the exception to the rule?

Luke was as different to Michael as chalk to cheese, she admitted. Michael was quiet, unassuming, totally dedicated and a worrier. His clean-cut looks, fair hair and hazel eyes had been the exact opposite of Luke's dark, provocative sensuality. The contrast was radical.

She'd had a crush on Michael at ten when her brother had first brought him home. Love of horses had often brought Michael to Collingwood, her parents' stud farm. It had seemed a natural progression for her to take the job Dick Shaw had offered her, of trainee veterinary nurse, when she left school. She'd considered working for her father at Collingwood, but the temptation of an all-rounder vets practice — and Michael of course — had made up her mind to accept.

No one was in the least surprised when at twenty she had married the boss's son. They were always Sophie and Mike, even when Michael was away training in London. No party invitation ever came without their twinned names.

For some reason, memories sprang unbidden into her mind as she dried herself. Time had a way of preserving the good, fading the bad, but the truth suddenly began to make its painful way to the surface as she slipped on her silk robe and stared into the mirror at her slim, wet-haired reflection.

The irony was, she had devoted every moment to the practice after Michael had gone. Yet hadn't his obsession for work driven a wedge between them when he was alive?

The mistake was in thinking she could change him. But it was she who had changed, smothering her want for a child, ignoring her clamouring instinct like a toothache that might go away in the end.

Sophie looked away abruptly, pressing the familiar guilt feelings back. Her eyes reflected too much tonight in the mirror and she wasn't ready yet to face it, whatever it was.

From her bedroom window she could see over to the darkened bungalow. Luke threatened her in some way, made her feel vulnerable . . . was he, however, a good vet? she asked herself as she peered through the glass.

She was forced to admit today had shown her he was. Siegfried, for instance. No one could have been more concerned or acted more ably than Luke. All her preconceptions of him had evaporated as he revived the old dog. He had cared deeply, enough for her to see another side of his character as he asserted himself with the disgruntled owner.

Howard had been correct; he was the right man for the practice. The problem was, she was having a hard time in accepting it.

* * *

The following morning Sophie discovered John Marks and Howard discussing the control of colic in horses. She eagerly joined in the discussion, unaware that Luke had walked into the room behind her.

'Ah, Luke!' Howard called brightly. 'Are you finding your feet?'

Luke strolled over, dressed impeccably in a crisp cream shirt and grey suit. 'With Sophie's excellent help,' he grinned. 'Without her yesterday, my case of congestive heart failure would have been far more traumatic than it turned out to be.'

'Sophie's wasted in administration,' Howard grunted. 'I've always thought we should have her back in surgery. She was Dick Shaw's right hand when he was alive.'

'I don't doubt it,' Luke replied, and she made herself look at him.

'I venture to disagree with you, Howard.' John Marks spoke. He was a young, eager and slightly over-intense locum, but Sophie liked him and hoped he would stay with the practice. Now he seemed to sense that Howard, in his usual forthright manner, had touched a raw nerve. 'Sophie's fine where she is, if you ask me. We'd all be a lot of loose cannons firing around the place without her direction.'

'I like her just the way she is,' Luke

observed wickedly.

Sophie flicked him a warning glance. She had vowed she would treat him no differently to John or Howard even if she had to wire her jaws to achieve it.

'Time I was in surgery,' Howard mumured tactfully.

'Me too,' John agreed, sifting papers into his case.

'I've two farms to haggle with this morning on swine vaccine.'

As the meeting broke up and Sophie began to make her way along the hall, Luke caught up with her. 'That conversation sounded interesting.'

She nodded. 'Yes, it was.'

'Which makes it even harder for me to upset the applecart,' he sighed, keeping in step with her.

She glanced at him under her lashes. 'What now?'

He put up both hands. 'Nothing to do with me this time, I promise. Lucy's father rang in. She had a fall yesterday evening from her mare. Right ankle's in plaster — he wanted to let you know she's OK, but the damage could be a problem regarding work for a few weeks.'

Sophie's heart sank. 'When did you take the message?

'Last night when you'd gone home. I knew there was nothing you could do and you'd probably have bitten my head off if I'd darkened your doorstep, so I left a note on your desk.'

Sophie walked in her office to find a spidery message scrawled on a sheet of paper balanced on the very top of her paperwork. She jerked her head up to find him gazing at her, the blue eyes amused.

'Sorry,' he shrugged, not looking sorry at all.

'It's not your fault,' she admitted, letting out a sigh of frustration. 'But it's annoying, to say the least.'

'Shall I come and console you?'

She lifted a warning eyebrow. 'Don't you dare step over that threshold. Heavens, I've enough to worry about with Lucy off now. Just when I thought we were beginning to surface.'

'Throw on your old nurse's uniform and I'll help you with the books. You can pay me overtime in kind.'

'You wish!' she muttered, picking up the phone to ring Lucy's number.

He shrugged and went to walk away. Suddenly she felt sorry she had taken her annoyance out on him and, before she dialled, held the phone over her shoulder. 'Are you comfortable in the bungalow?' she called to make up for her snapped reply.

He stopped in his tracks. 'Ah, I knew you cared.'

'Don't push your luck,' she grinned. 'I was only asking.'

He sauntered back into the room. 'Well, as a matter of fact, the lights all fused last night. My knowledge of electrical wiring is limited to a very basic DIY, so, not unexpectedly, it took me all of a couple of hours to discover where the fault lay and drive into Cranthorpe for fuse-wire.'

'You should have asked. I have some at the house.'

'I considered it,' he confessed, 'especially when I saw a shadow at your bedroom window. In fact I thought about hopping over straight away.'

'I'll bet you did,' she giggled, unable to help her amusement. 'Are the lights OK now?'

'Seem to be. Do you want to come and test them?'

'Get lost,' she threw at him, returning to the chore of dialling Lucy.

A few minutes later she sat considering her options. Perhaps Luke had a point. She could take home in the evening all the bookwork she couldn't do during the day, and take Lucy's place temporarily. It might work without having to search for a temporary nurse.

Her answer came more rapidly than expected when at five-thirty the next morning the phone shrieked beside her.

Luke's voice came over the line as she fumbled to waken. 'Dreaming of me I hope?' he asked cheerfully.

She kicked her legs out of bed. 'Luke.

46

What's the matter?'

'Rise and shine, my pretty one — I need help.'

'At this hour of the morning?' She squinted at her bedside clock. 'You're joking!'

'Unfortunately not. Tom Grayshot is a client of John's. He was walking with his retriever this morning when she bolted after a squirrel into the path of a motorcyle. Grayshot said it only clipped her leg, but the X-rays show a fracture. I'm going to set it — like to help?'

An offer she accepted immediately, knowing that the setting would be best carried out by two pairs of hands. In a few minutes she had slithered on jeans and T-shirt, discounting make-up because of the time factor.

Arriving breathlessly at the practice, she almost ran into Luke in the prep-room tying his green scrubs behind his back. He whistled through his teeth. 'Now it is a good morning!'

'How's the patient?' Sophie gasped, avoiding the blue eyes which homed in

47

over her slender T-shirted figure.

'Not bad, considering.' He leaned against the sink, assessing her with lazy blue eyes. 'Did anyone ever tell you you barely look eighteen without make-up on?'

She turned away, conscious of her freshened cheeks and fair-lashed eyes still drowsy with sleep. She glanced in the theatre at the dog that lay on the operating table. 'How did it happen?' she persisted, frowning.

Luke sighed, returning his attention to pulling on his surgical gloves. 'The rider didn't stop, which infuriated the farmer the most. Luckily they weren't too far from his farm, so he picked her up, returned to his Land Rover and brought her straight here.'

'Internal injuries?' Sophie frowned as she unfolded a fresh surgical gown.

'No concussion or internal injuries; just the leg. Fortunately she'd not eaten, so I was able to anaesthetise her and take X-rays.'

'And the farmer?'

'I took his number and told him we'd ring later on. Like to see the X-rays?'

Studying them, Sophie saw it was clear that the honey-coloured retriever on the operating table had sustained more of an injury than the farmer suggested.

'As you can see, they reveal a comminuted fracture line . . . here, a mid-shaft fracture of the tibia and fibula. God, you smell gorgeous. What is it?' he asked, bending to sniff her hair.

Sophie moved back. 'Luke, can we please concentrate?'

'I'll try,' he grunted. 'But you're making me dizzy with that perfume.'

'I haven't any on. There wasn't any time — remember?' She was uncomfortably aware of his warm body next to her, the brush of his arm against hers, the *frisson* of black hair scattered in abundance across the hard muscle of his arms, tickling her skin.

He grinned with a flash of white teeth.

'What about cuts or lacerations?' She

averted her gaze, keeping her eyes studiously on the X-ray.

'Grazes; nothing that needs stitching, luckily. No broken pieces of bone either, which would have complicated things.' He pointed to a sterile pack on the work bench. 'I've decided to use a method of external fixation for repair — a Schroeder Thomas extension splint. Are you familiar with the technique, by any chance — or is that a silly question?'

Sophie smiled smugly. 'Yes, I'm quite familiar with the Schroeder Thomas,' she told him, glancing down at the lightweight aluminium rod he had formed into an external frame.

He turned his eyes up to the ceiling. 'It was a silly question. Well, let's get a move-on.'

As the fracture repair progressed she was not for an instant disappointed with the way he worked. He was, as Howard had judged, an excellent surgeon, skilfully immobilising the fracture and applying the splint.

Knowing what was required, she carefully assisted him with the angle of Josie's foot, wrapping and suspending it with zinc oxide tape, attaching it to the bar so the dog would have enough support.

He worked swiftly as he placed a well-padded protective ring gently against the pubic region. Stopping chafing was important, but not always included in the hurry to plaster. As Sophie applied Nappi-Roll in the form of a padded sling around the leg she was aware Luke had not forgotten the ring, a small but important kindness in the care of his patient.

He took a step back and nodded. 'We'll seal the whole thing with stock plaster. She's lucky not to have had any bacterial contamination — the only danger is a callus might form, so I'll want to keep a weekly check on her.'

Sophie nodded. 'I'll block out an appointment each week for her. The trouble with farmers is, they are apt to get so busy and forget things like appointments.'

Luke arched dark eyebrows. 'Then let's keep her in for a bit and I'll check the fracture immobilisation until I'm sure she's OK.'

Sophie smiled. 'I had a feeling that's what you'd say.'

'Reading my mind already?' he teased. 'What else can you read there?'

She flipped off her white dusted gloves with a wry smile. 'Nothing I'd care to repeat.'

He turned amused blue eyes on her as she began to help him fix the drip. 'You're spoiling my fun again.'

'You need a breakfast, not fun,' she grinned as they lifted Josie and her drip into Recovery.

'Why don't you come and share one with me?' he asked hopefully as he joined her to flip on the tap in the prep-room. 'I'm a pretty fair hand at scrambled eggs and bacon.'

She shook her head, soaping her hands under the hot water. 'Coffee and the post is my next stop.'

He handed her a towel and as she grasped it his large hands came over hers, taking each finger to dry them individually, rubbing the tips gently, making a slow, circular movement across the palms with the cloth.

She tried to drag them away, heart in mouth, but somehow his fingers searched out each crease and crevice until, satisfied he'd dried them, he let her go.

'Don't tell me you didn't enjoy that?' he grinned.

'I — '

'Sophie, don't fib.'

'I . . . I wasn't going to — '

In the silence of the empty rooms she thought she could hear her heartbeat, driving against her ribs as the palms slid coaxingly down her bare arms.

'Luke . . . don't,' she whispered.

'Why not?' He frowned, the heavy-lidded eyes puzzled. 'You're attracted to me and I'm attracted to you. A perfectly healthy situation, or at least it would be if you didn't keep denying it.'

'I'm not denying anything,' she answered with surprising calm. 'The question of attraction hasn't even arisen.'

'Now you are fibbing!' He pulled her closer.

Sophie put her hands on his chest to stop him, realising with a jolt she didn't want him to stop. She gave a little push and, to her surprise, he let her go.

'See you at nine,' he shrugged, collecting his sweater from a hook. 'Workaholic!'

A description she found herself secretly relating to as she hurried to fetch the morning's post and examine it in the privacy of her office.

As she sank into her seat Steamer lifted his head from the position he always occupied under the desk and licked her hand. Sighing, she rested back. 'Good dog,' she murmured distractedly, aware that her thoughts were still in the prep-room.

She had been tempted to let him kiss

her. Fool. She shouldn't be taking his behaviour seriously; he obviously just couldn't help himself.

Deep in thought, she almost jumped out of her seat when the door shot open. 'By the way,' Luke called, his blue eyes twinkling as he looked across the room, 'leave Saturday evening free. I've a table booked at the Moathouse in Cranthorpe for eight-thirty.'

Her brown eyes flew open. 'What did you just say?'

'Supper, some sexy conversation — '

'No way!'

He stood with his hands on his hips, the soft dark linen trousers moulding to his long legs. 'All work and no play makes Sophie a very dull girl.'

'Then I'll be dull if I like,' she snapped crossly, 'but it's my business and mine alone.'

'Now you have hurt my feelings.' He pulled a face.

'Your feelings!' Sophie stared at him incredulously. 'What about mine?'

'I'm just teasing,' he admitted as he

watched the horror spread over her face. 'You're not coming out with me alone. You're coming out with Howard and Molly and me, the four of us. It's their anniversary, apparently.'

Somewhere in the back of her mind a bell rang. 'I'd forgotten,' she muttered, still bewildered. 'But why should Howard and Molly want us to go with them?'

He shrugged again. 'Who was I to refuse when Howard suggested the idea?'

'You could have asked me.'

'You would have said no.'

She felt as if she needed to throw something at him but he dived from the room before she reached for the only available object, a china mug.

Then suddenly a thought occurred to her. Why believe him? Neither Howard nor Molly had mentioned this. Perhaps it was his idea of a joke.

She idly fingered the letter she had almost screwed up in her hand. Looking down at it, she recognised the writing. Molly Oliver had written a few sentences saying she hoped Sophie and Luke would be able to join them for a celebratory dinner at the Moathouse on Saturday, their thirty-fifth anniversary. Howard would probably forget to mention it, the post-script said, hence the letter.

Sophie covered her face with her hands. If it meant sabotaging the plumbing and instigating a flood as an excuse for not going, it would be worth it just to get the upper hand on Luke Jordon.

3

By Saturday afternoon however, Sophie had neither orchestrated a flood nor developed flu. She had twice broached the topic of the dinner to Howard and twice been unable to provide a reasonable excuse.

Since Luke had skilfully avoided a confrontation with her Sophie found herself gazing into her wardrobe with frantic eyes. She loved dressing for an occasion, something she had rarely done over the last two years. For work she always took the utmost care to look smart, wearing designer suits, projecting, she hoped, a good image for the practice.

The chance to dress tonight did appeal . . . but not for Luke's benefit. For two pins she'd pick up the phone and cancel now if it wasn't for Howard's and Molly's anniversary.

She showered and washed her hair and slid on ivory silk underwear against her scented skin. This was the first time she had socialised without Michael — not that eating out had been high on their list of priorities; the practice had been too all-consuming. The theatre, dancing, holidays . . . they had all gradually evaporated in the wake of work.

Sophie locked the thoughts from her mind. She didn't want to remember the shadows of her marriage — shadows disappeared if you let them fade away.

She gazed critically into the mirror. The silk dress she had chosen was a rich shade of claret. It bore witness to her slender figure. If she had lost weight over the last two years, then now it appeared to have been regained in the right places, her feminine breasts curved and full under the smooth material.

Since the early May evening was breezy, she slipped on a chiffon blouson in a deeper shade of claret. Lastly she threaded golden loops into her ears beneath her blonde hair.

Luke was prompt. Eight on the dot. Immaculate black dinner suit, flawless white shirt, black bow tie. He looked stunning.

'Is this all for me?' The blue eyes widened as they moved over her.

'No,' she grinned, clutching her bag. 'We're celebrating for Molly and Howard tonight — remember?'

'Speak for yourself,' he sighed under his breath, attempting to close the door behind him. 'I know what I'm celebrating — '

Sophie dashed to catch the door. 'I'm ready to go.'

He made a low swoop with his arm. 'Madam's chariot awaits her.'

Steamer nuzzled into her cheek as she bent to pat him, then rubbed against Luke's long legs. As Sophie walked out he bent to ruffle the dog's soft black coat. 'Hold the fort, laddie,' she heard him say softly.

'Well, who'd have believed it?' Luke

grinned as he started the Jaguar.

'Believed what?' Sophie frowned across at him.

'That I'd finally get you out for some supper and sexy conversation.'

'You haven't. Molly and Howard have,' she stressed.

'You can't talk to them all night,' he assured her. 'I'm bound to get a little attention.'

She sat quietly, smiling. 'You never tire, do you?'

'Of what?'

'Of fooling around, of course.'

'I'll have you know I'm deadly serious,' he informed her indignantly. 'What makes you think I'm fooling around?'

She shrugged. 'You're so good at it.'

He grinned. 'Comes with practice.'

'Don't boast,' she laughed, 'and watch where you're driving.'

'It's hard to watch anything else when you're beside me.'

She lifted her eyebrows. 'You see? You just can't help it. This chat-up line. It's as if you're in overdrive all the time.'

His profile sobered innocently. 'I'm not chatting you up. I'm having fun with you, which is an entirely different thing. And you're having fun with me, though you won't admit it.'

He was right, she thought guiltily, turning her face to the window. She was enjoying herself. She hadn't laughed so much in a long while. He had that effect on her, but then, he probably did on most women.

The Moathouse in Cranthorpe had been built in the last eighteen months, a stark contrast to the old traditional buildings, and its modern pale brick and brightly lit windows welcomed them as they drew up.

'There's Howard's car,' Luke said. 'Looks like we won't have time for our quiet little cocktail.'

'You're driving anyway,' Sophie reminded him ruefully.

'Do you never break any rules?' he teased.

'Never.'

He grinned. 'Saint Sophie.'

A remark she chose to ignore as they walked in and were shown to their table. Molly Oliver embraced Sophie and she caught a whiff of Molly's perennial Lily of the Valley.

'At last we've persuaded you out,' Molly laughed, patting her grey, freshly washed and blow-dried hair.

'Not us.' Howard kissed Sophie on the cheek. 'You can thank Luke for bringing her out of hibernation.'

Sophie flushed, realising that tonight's gesture had sprung from the well-intentioned Olivers. They had often tried to persuade her out over the past two years, but with little success. Luke had probably told her the truth when he said Howard had connived the whole thing, and now she felt rather sorry that he had probably been roped into the evening too.

Though older now, Sophie reflected that the Olivers had changed little over the years. She had known them both since she was fifteen and her Saturday job at the surgery. They were devoted to the practice, Molly herself an ex-nurse. In the last few years they had weathered the demise of both their oldest friend and partner Dick Shaw, and of his son Michael.

Sadly she felt that after Michael's death Howard really hadn't the same enthusiasm for the practice.

The meal was sumptuous; king-prawn cocktail for starters, slivers of beef flamed in wine at the table, accompanied by fresh vegetables and finally a crème caramel, the house speciality, lost in fresh cream.

'I think I've put on at least half a stone,' Molly sighed when the last morsel was gone from her plate. She reached for her husband's hand. 'Happy anniversary, darling.'

'A toast,' Luke said, raising his glass, 'to you both.' His glass touched Sophie's. 'To the future.'

'Seconded,' Howard echoed, and Sophie avoided Luke's gaze as she sipped the champagne.

Suddenly a man dressed in a white tuxedo sat at the grand piano on the far side of the restaurant. 'Oh, Cole Porter . . . let's dance,' sighed Molly, dragging a reluctant Howard onto the dance-floor.

'Enjoying yourself?' Luke asked when they were alone.

Sophie nodded. 'They're a great couple, aren't they?'

'You all go back a long way, don't you?'

'Not that we ever had time to come out like this,' Sophie reflected honestly. 'There was always so much to do. Either Michael or Howard on call . . .'

'A big mistake,' Luke sighed. 'Work is an easy trap to fall into. Your priorities become blurred, and even one's identity — so much so that you wake up one day and wonder who you are. Mostly, you are other people's property. Not much left for yourself if you're not careful.'

'It wasn't like that with us,' she heard herself defending too quickly.

He frowned at her. 'At the risk of having my head bitten off, I'd say the practice was in danger of overtaking your personal lives.'

'No!'

His hand touched her shoulder. 'Admitting the truth isn't a hanging offence.'

'We may have had different goals,' she mumbled reluctantly. 'Michael was dedicated to the practice — and I suppose I . . . I . . . wanted a family.'

'And Michael didn't.'

Her mouth opened to protest but she found it impossible to lie, her eyes blurring as she looked down at her hands clenched in her lap.

'People want different things as they grow,' he said gently. 'We're human, each with our own ideas and sometimes they don't match with those of our loved ones. Especially loved ones. I suppose that's why I'm a confirmed bachelor. Selfishly I prefer my own preconceptions of life to anyone else's.'

The music suddenly stopped and

Howard and Molly came back to the table, laughing and breathless. 'Why don't you two dance?' Molly suggested as she tumbled into her seat.

'Oh, I don't think — ' Sophie began as Luke took hold of her hand. Under the rueful gaze of the Olivers, he pulled her to the dance-floor.

'I'm out of practice,' she mumbled as she stood stiffly, then felt him bring her towards him, discovering that in her high heels she seemed to perfectly fit into the curve of his long body.

'There, you see? No problem,' he whispered, drawing her close. 'And now let your hips loosen,' he whispered, his hands gently bringing the small of her back towards him. 'See how easy it is? Like riding a bike.'

He nudged her soft blonde hair with his lips, pressing her breasts against his chest. 'Now, why didn't we do this in the first place?' he murmured huskily. 'It would have solved all our communication problems.'

An answer failed to materialise as she

closed her eyes and slid her arms around his neck. She felt the heat of his fingers slide over the silk of her dress, felt his heart and hers beating as one. Aroused, confused and feeling helpless, she gave herself up to the flood-tide of sensation which flowed through her.

The music was soft and soothing. The tunes changed, each one more romantic than the other, going from Broadway hits to recent love songs. She was barely conscious of the changing in melodies, for Luke's guidance of her around the floor was so slow and subtle that she felt in another world.

He murmured, 'Do you know, this is the first time I've seen you relax?'

She made a mumbled response, her nerve-ends tingling in every part of her body.

'Come closer,' he whispered, his soft breath catching her face. 'Like this . . . ' He brought her to his chest, running his fingers down her back.

She put up no resistance. Melting into his strong body was so, so easy. His breath on her hair, the beating of his heart under her breast, the rhythmic movement of his hard thighs against hers . . .

'I'm afraid the music's stopped, my sweet,' he whispered some time later. To her desperate shame, she realised they were alone on the floor. She snatched her arms from his neck, peeling herself away from him, her cheeks going scarlet.

'I — er — won't be long,' she mumbled, deciding that a visit to the loo was appropriate.

Her legs were shaking as she entered the pretty rose-pink room and sank onto a stool, staring at her fevered reflection in the mirror.

Why did he bring out these sensations in her? Why did she feel so scared, so excited, so bewildered all at once?

Stooping to press cold water on her face from the tap, she stared again at her flushed face in the mirror.

Luke was a hopeless flirt, a rake. He made her laugh, and tonight, when he had made her admit to wanting a child, he made her want to cry. He had also impressed on her he was a confirmed bachelor — and she needed no convincing.

In which case, why did she feel like this? Knowing what he was had not prevented her from feeling weak with desire on the dance-floor. She had responded to the strength and agility of his body as she had wrapped her hands around his neck, felt herself quiver as the hard thigh muscles had touched against hers, impelling her to hold tighter to the strong shoulder muscles.

By the time she had composed herself and looked again into the mirror she saw huge brown eyes gazing back. Eyes she barely recognised because of their intensity, set over high, curving cheekbones, a waterfall wave of golden-blonde hair falling over her cheek. She saw what she didn't want to see; she looked like a woman who had already embarked on an adulterous affair. But the love of her life was dead.

And she had no intention of starting an affair!

⋆   ⋆   ⋆

The slender figure standing beside Luke at their table was a perfect stranger. She was a tall, dark-haired girl, very young, not more than twenty.

'Sophie,' Luke said as he rose from his seat, 'I'd like you to meet a friend of mine, Amanda Drew.'

Realising the girl had already been introduced to Howard and Molly, she smiled, noting the long nut-brown hair which swept down around her very bare shoulders.

'Will you join us, Mandy?' Luke asked.

The girl hesitated. 'Thanks, but I won't. Tonight I'm with friends but I'll call by to see you next week.' She smiled at the assembled company and left to join a small group who waited at the restaurant exit.

Sophie sat down in her seat. She

glanced at Luke, watching his gaze follow the slender figure.

Howard leant forward. 'Have you enjoyed yourself, my dear?'

She nodded. 'It's been a lovely evening, Howard. The meal was perfect.'

Luke agreed too. But the atmosphere had changed. He seemed to lose interest in the conversation, his eyes not meeting hers as he returned his attention, with difficulty, to the table.

* * *

Sophie felt her cheeks crimson as she recalled her thoughts in the cloakroom last night. It was only luck which had brought her to her senses. If she hadn't met Amanda Drew, so obviously involved with Luke by the way she had looked at him, then she dreaded to think where her befuddled brain might have landed her.

Not that Luke had explained after taking leave of the Olivers. Delivering her safely to her doorstep, he'd merely bent to kiss her briefly on the cheek and then left.

Humiliation had burned in her cheeks as she'd tried to sleep. Convincing herself he couldn't have known what a chaos of emotions he'd provoked, sleep had finally come in the early hours.

At eight she stared from her window at the rain. Sunday yawned ahead. As always, work was the answer. She dashed to the practice in her cagoule after breakfast to make inroads into the paperwork. Irresistible was the urge as she made coffee to glance through the rain-lashed office window to the bungalow.

The storm, she noticed, had taken the heads from the flowers, driving them across the lawn. The path leading to Luke's front door was strewn with leaves. There was no sign of Luke or the Jaguar.

Sunday ended on a burst of thunder. Hail cut swaths across a purple sky, and after checking Siegfried and Josie, who would later be fed and exercised by the duty nurse, Sophie dashed with Steamer from the practice back home.

It wasn't until the early hours that the storm blew itself out. Next morning she dressed in a summer-blue suit to befit the brilliant sun now rebelliously shining on a rain-soaked earth.

'Any news from Lucy?' Jane enquired as she arrived in Reception.

'Nothing new.' Sophie shrugged as she glanced at the appointments book, her head only to jerk up as the door flew open.

'You aren't going to believe this,' Luke announced as he stood in jeans and wellies, flicking soggy bits from his shirt.

Both girls stared.

'The lounge roof fell in last night.' He presented them with a damp piece of plaster as evidence.

'The roof?' they echoed, staring at it.

'I've cleared a bit of the mess but it's going to be one heck of a job.'

'Were you sitting under it?' Jane gasped.

Luke brushed white flecks from his hair as he grinned. 'You'd have been visiting me in hospital if I had. Luckily I was away. Didn't find the roof on the floor till I came home.'

'First the wiring and now this,' Sophie sighed.

Luke shrugged. 'I don't think the place likes me.' Two early clients pushed their way by, staring at his dishevelled state. 'I'd better change,' he frowned, 'before I scare everyone off.'

Sophie put up a hand. 'Er — do you need anything?'

'What are you offering?' he mouthed teasingly.

Jane giggled.

'Not what you're thinking!' Sophie mumbled crossly.

As he disappeared her mind flew ahead to all the new problems which were now posed, among them, would the bungalow be habitable? If not, where would he live? With difficulty she stopped herself from assuming the worst — perhaps the room could be replastered.

A quarter of an hour later Luke appeared at her office door dressed in a fresh blue cotton shirt and dark blue cords. 'If you're sitting there worrying about me, don't,' he called cheerfully.

She had been trying to read a report. It was, as he guessed, useless trying to concentrate.

'I've booked a room at the Cranthorpe Arms while the repairs are on,' he told her with a dismissive wave of his hand.

'But it's a pub!' she protested, her brown eyes widening.

He shrugged. 'The food comes highly recommended and I'm sure the beds are cockroach-free.'

'You can't,' she protested weakly.

He bent forward and rested his palms on her desk. 'Do I have a better offer from the lady with the large brown eyes and sexy smile?'

Sophie's jaw dropped. 'You mean — my place?'

'Why not? I'll pay rent.'

She looked stricken. He burst out with laughter. 'Don't worry, I wouldn't dream of it. Good grief, what would the neighbours say?'

She stood up. 'It wasn't a question of the neighbours — '

'I was only joking.' He laughed at her evident dismay. 'Stop fretting, Sophie. I shall be quite happy at the pub; don't worry about it.'

'But I do,' she blurted. 'Er — after all, your contract says . . . '

'As much as I love talking with you, my sweet, I have to go. I'm on call and Hollybrook Farm have rung in. As a matter of fact, I haven't a clue where it is yet.'

Sophie thought for a moment. 'Wait, I know where it is. I'll come with you.'

'Will wonders never cease?' he gasped in exaggerated surprise.

She filed the report and switched off her terminal. 'Hollybrook Farm is down the road from the builders who helped us convert the practice. I'll call in and ask them to come to the bungalow. With any luck, I may be able to persuade them to come right away.'

He grinned as she hurried past him. 'See what my threat to move in with you caused — instant solution to the problem.'

She stopped and sighed. 'Luke, I was rude. In an emergency you would have been welcome to stay at my place.'

He laughed and took her arm. 'I'm all for emergencies. Give me time and I'll soon think of one.'

★　★　★

Luke slipped on his waterproof gown and examined the poor creature that Kenny Hines had penned in his yard.

He ran his hand over the distended flank and painfully arched back of the bloated black and white cow. 'I'm going to have to empty her stomach, Mr Hines, and get rid of whatever is in there. I'll do it by drench, so I'd like plenty of water, please.'

Kenny Hines hurried off and Sophie glanced at her watch as she stood in the yard. Not realising the cow would need drenching, they had stopped here first before going on to the builders.

'I'll also need Epsom Salts,' Luke added as he withdrew his gloved hand from the cow, 'and possibly liquid paraffin. I've plenty in the Jag. Do you mind nipping back and getting it for me, Sophie?'

She nodded, giving up hope that this would be a swift operation. She knew cows of old and as a precaution she opened the boot of his car, pulling out the proverbial spare overalls and a pair of extra-large boots. Quickly slipping into the back of the Jaguar, she slid off her skirt and top and put on the overalls, fetching Luke's equipment before she hurried back to the pen.

Luke and Kenny greeted her with surprise. Luke grinned, taking the bag from her. 'Overalls become you, Mrs

Shaw,' he said as his fingers held hers just for a split-second on the bag. 'And boots too.'

Trying to dismiss an involuntary lurch of her stomach muscles as the blue eyes teased her, she cast her gaze to the cow. 'Trocar and cannula?' she asked, referring to the dagger-like implement and thin metal sheath used for cow bloat.

Luke nodded. 'Now why did I have the feeling you were going to suggest that?'

Sophie grinned. 'I'll help.'

'OK by me.' Luke glanced at the farmer. 'No need to hang about, Mr Hines. I've all the help I need now, thanks.'

The farmer gazed sceptically at Sophie's slender though overclothed form and reluctantly left his cow in their hands, frowning back over his shoulder.

Between them, they began the drenching. With the oil and stimulants administered by mouth, Luke plunged the implement into the skin, piercing the rumen, relieving the animal instantly of its uncomfortable tension. After a while, helped along by the oral stimulants, the rumen began to resume its normal duties.

'Watch out!' Luke called and, jumping aside, Sophie narrowly missed the evacuation, glancing up at Luke, who was trying hard to control his mirth.

She groaned, staring at her caked boots and splattered overalls. 'I suppose you think that's funny?'

Luke nodded, but was caught by an unexpected movement himself.

'Serves you right!' She laughed so much as he squelched backwards that she felt the tears run down her cheeks. She wiped them with the back of her hand, smearing dirt and mascara together.

Luke grinned at her dirty face and baggy trousers. 'You look like Charlie Chaplin,' he laughed. But she allowed him to rub his handkerchief across her nose and cheeks, noting with satisfaction that it was black when he returned it to his overall pocket.

'Tell you what you need now,' he said with a devious smirk. She saw him dash to the nearby shed and emerge carrying a stiff-bristled broom.

'Oh, just what I've always wanted,' she sighed in mock gratitude as he waved it at her.

'Be careful what you wish for — you might just get it,' he whispered mischievously in her ear and she growled at him, tugging the broom from his hands.

She swept, reflecting that she was beginning to think more and more of what she wanted these days and, to her shame, it had very little to do with the practice, her eyes roaming to the neat, tight bottom above the never-ending legs as Luke bent to the underside of the penned cow.

Suddenly he swivelled around, his blue eyes catching hers. 'Naughty, naughty,' he teased, wagging a finger, and she turned away to hide her embarrassment.

Kenny Hines's wife Dora made the tea in the farmhouse kitchen and presented Luke with a bottle of Best Elderwine, made in the cellar of Hollybrook Farm. Sophie sat with Dora, having stowed away their dirty overalls in the Jaguar after changing in the Hines's downstairs cloakroom.

'Take my tip,' Dora said with a wink as she poured a second cup, 'he's not a bad catch, that one. Kenny said he knows his job all right. Bloat's gone down already.'

Sophie flushed. She didn't know what Dora meant as far as catches went. Presuming it was a compliment to Luke's efficiency and the luck of the practice to have him, she merely nodded, savouring the warm dark tea as she drank.

It didn't escape her notice, though, that Dora nudged Kenny in the ribs as they left. The Hineses had been on their books for a decade and remembered the Shaws. Sophie fought with the different sensations Dora's reaction had evoked. Trying to sort them out just gave her a headache and she sighed as Luke drove into the builder's yard.

Luke brought the car to a halt, turning to catch her sigh. He was dressed in his blue cords and shirt again, the few buttons undone at the neck, revealing to Sophie's sensitive eyes a thick forest of jet-black chest hair.

'That'll teach you to accompany a vet on a bloat case,' he laughed beside her.

She smiled ruefully. 'It . . . was fun.'

He said slowly, 'Yes . . . it was.'

She laughed. 'Beware the monster you've created.'

'Oh, I get the blame, do I?'

She glanced at him, giggling. 'No, we can blame Kenny's cow this time.'

He met her eyes and there was a hesitant silence between them before he looked back at the road. 'Let's hear what Ted Frost has to say about the roof.'

She sighed, coming back down to earth. 'Yes, I suppose so.'

'Cheer up,' he shrugged. 'I'm sure it will be OK.'

Sophie wasn't so sure. What she hadn't told Luke was that the bungalow had needed an overhaul two years ago. It was the last of the properties associated with the practice to require attention, and yet after Michael's death she had put it off for the simple reason that it so often remained empty, the occasional locum vet using it when accommodation proved scarce in Cranthorpe. Now she bitterly regretted the omission.

However, Ted Frost didn't seem too worried when they described the problem. A big, burly man in his mid-fifties, he had been a friend of her father-in-law's and was helpful to a point, promising to come the next day.

They took their leave and drove back past Hollybrook Farm. 'Would you like a snack in town?' Luke asked, glancing at his watch.

She glanced at the time and shook her head. 'It's half-one and I've some drug-house reps to see at two.'

'That gives us half an hour,' Luke pointed out. 'Enough time for a shandy and a sandwich somewhere. Be a devil, break the rules for once.'

She shook her head. 'I told you, I don't break them.'

'Sophie, you — ' he began and then shrugged, frowning back at the road as he edged the Jaguar through the crowded streets of Cranthorpe.

They were soon at the practice and Luke parked the Jaguar next to her Volvo estate. He pulled on the brake, but as she went to get out he held her arm. 'You know, you're going to burn yourself out, the rate you're going,' he told her gently.

A stirring of resentment went through her. 'If I am, it's my business, Luke. But I know what I'm doing, even if you think I don't.'

He shook his head slowly. 'You want everything perfect, Sophie — the practice, your staff and, most of all, yourself. Your standards are crippling. Have you ever taken time to think why?'

The accusation stunned her into silence.

'Guilt,' he said simply. 'Guilt over something you can't do anything about; the past. You want everything right, as Michael would have had it. You've taken on his mantle.'

'Th-that's not true,' she bleated, furious at his intrusion.

'Don't you realise you were acting as any woman would act, wanting a baby? It wasn't wrong. Michael didn't die because you wanted a child. He died in an accident. End of story. It can happen to anyone, any time.'

'I've heard enough — ' She thrust her hand against the door and before he could stop her she was running across the car park, tears in her eyes.

She hated him for talking about Michael, for telling her how she was behaving. She hated it. And, as she hurried to the side-entrance to avoid meeting anyone else, she hated him most, because what he said held the painful ring of truth.

4

'This is Maroc and I'd like him to have a full health check,' an attractive brunette said that afternoon as she stood in Reception accompanied by a silver-haired borzoi. 'I'd like Maroc to be treated by Luke Jordon. Is he here?'

Luke had set out on more calls and Sophie, who was manning the desk, glanced at the appointments book. 'He's on his visits this afternoon, I'm afraid.'

'You're Mrs Shaw, aren't you?' Black manicured eyebrows pleated together in a frown. 'I'm Patricia De Vere. I expect Luke has mentioned me?'

Patricia De Vere was about to speak again when her attention faltered. Two young men, tall and well dressed, strode into Reception, briefcases in hand.

Jane appeared at the same time,

recognising the pharmaceutical representatives. 'Shall I take over here while you attend to James and Hamish?' she asked, glancing at the unfamiliar woman.

Curiosity held in restraint, Sophie nodded. 'A health check for Mrs De Vere's dog — with Luke, please,' she said pointedly. 'And then will you ring Mrs Farley and tell her she can come in to collect Siegfried later today?'

At her sign, James and Hamish followed Sophie along to the office and very soon were deep into discussion, though she couldn't help wondering about the mysterious dark-haired visitor and her elegant borzoi.

She had known James and Hamish for several years, relying on their helpfulness with the ordering of drugs — Hamish even delivering them himself when one of the vets requested an urgent order.

James departed first after having made his list and finally Hamish rose to pack his case, several empty mugs of coffee in evidence on the desk. 'One last request,' he grinned as he walked to the door.

'Your order book's crammed . . . don't be greedy, Hamish Burns!' she laughed.

'No, no more orders, but dinner is long overdue — just name the day.'

Sophie understood this was not a personal invitation, for Hamish extended the offer on behalf of his firm. 'You'll get me the sack if my bosses think I've no charm for my clients,' he warned her with a rueful grin.

'I'll give it some thought, I promise,' she relented, walking to the door and opening it, 'but at the moment I can't move for the backlog of work.'

Hamish lifted his bushy blond eyebrows, the same straw colour as his thick curly hair, in defeat. At that moment Luke appeared, his eyes taking in Sophie and the young man beside her.

'Oh, Luke, this is Hamish Burns, our pharmaceutical brains,' she introduced.

The two men shook hands and Sophie was surprised to note their distanced nods before Hamish left.

Afterwards Luke walked along the hall with her. 'You seem like old friends,' he commented drolly.

Sophie stopped, remembering the earlier visitor. 'Yes, we are — which reminds me. A Mrs Patricia De Vere and her borzoi named Maroc came in to see you just after lunch.'

Luke lifted an eyebrow. 'The dog unwell?'

Sophie hesitated. 'Not as far as I know. She asked for a full health check for him and Jane made an appointment.'

Luke nodded. 'Trish is an old friend from way back. The dog's probably in good enough shape.'

Why, then, the appointment? Sophie wondered. But before she could speak Luke nodded to Reception. 'Mrs Farley.'

'You did say you were ready for Siegfried to leave, didn't you?' she asked uncertainly.

Luke nodded. 'He's into his third day of digoxin. We can't keep the animal forever.'

'My husband thinks all this is quite unnecessary,' were Mrs Farley's first words as they met her.

Luke frowned. 'I should like to have spoken to your husband, but, as it seems unlikely, I must stress that the major effect of heart failure is the congestive accumulation of fluid in the body tissues. Siegfried needs rest and the prescribed medication.'

'Which is what?' demanded the woman.

'I've put him on a diuretic, which increases water loss via the kidneys,' Luke told her calmly, 'and I've added another drug to relieve respiratory signs of his disease.'

'My husband won't like it at all. He gives Siegfried seaweed pills and royal jelly.'

'As a supplementary — fine,' Luke agreed. 'But if Siegfried doesn't have the medication I have prescribed and his exercise is not reduced he is at risk from another heart attack.'

Jane brought Siegfried into the waiting-room and again Sophie sensed Luke's reticence to let him go. But there was nothing they could do except offer the advice and hope it would be taken.

'Damn,' Luke muttered when Mrs Farley had departed. 'There was nothing else I could do.'

Sophie was touched by his concern. Rarely had she seen anything get to him, but in this case she understood his frustration and completely agreed. 'I can't understand how people think in those terms,' she sighed. 'Don't they realise we're here to help?'

'Most do, thank God.' Luke tucked Siegfried's folder neatly together, lifting his brows to the noise of a diesel engine outside. 'Tom Grayshot,' he nodded as a farm van chugged by.

In stark contrast to the previous client, the farmer and his dog inspected one another rapturously. 'Little beauty, isn't she?' Farmer Grayshot sighed as Josie balanced on three legs.

'A way to go yet,' Luke reminded him. 'Actually the fourth leg is a spare, did you know that? Dogs can manage perfectly well on three, little terriers I've seen actually making do on two.'

The farmer laughed. 'Tell that to my cows, will you? Darned things refuse to get up if they feel so inclined.'

After the man and his dog had made a follow-up appointment and taken their leave Luke thrust a hand through his hair. 'I suppose we'd better break the news about the bungalow to Howard.'

Howard's reaction was of abject horror as they stood in the bungalow. The hole in the lounge ceiling allowed a view through to the rafters. Every room was covered in a film of thick white dust.

'It's much worse than I thought,' Sophie sighed desperately.

'It grows on you,' Luke joked, but no one laughed.

'You obviously can't stay here,' Howard groaned. 'You must come to us,' he went on to suggest, even though Sophie knew Molly looked after their daughter's children while she worked.

'Thanks all the same, but I've booked a room at the Cranthorpe Arms,' Luke refused politely.

'Burnt pie and soggy chips,' Howard muttered grimly.

'At least . . . come for a meal this evening,' Sophie heard herself saying as both men stared at her in surprise.

Howard laughed. 'I should snap the offer up,' he chuckled as Sophie went a bright pink.

* * *

There was nothing wrong, Sophie told herself, in Luke coming to dinner. Mysteriously, the idea of entertaining, after so long, burgeoned into certain terror that the meal would be a disaster.

Experience had shown her she was a good cook. On the long evenings

Michael had spent in surgery or on calls cooking had been a bolthole for her, her freezer a treasure trove of goodies — as it still was now when she managed to find time to keep it stocked.

A dish of freshly stir-fried chicken and walnuts on the hotplate, a banana cheesecake swiftly removed from the freezer and cream whipped and chilled, Sophie later realised her fears were groundless, at least for the meal.

With a half an hour to spare, she showered and dressed in a sleeveless white silk blouse, with tiny pearl buttons and plain beige culottes. Blonde hair swept back from her face in a smooth chignon, the first thing Luke said as he arrived was, predictably, 'Delicious!' — not referring to the food.

Sophie clutched the bottle he presented her with, frowning at the expensive label. 'I wouldn't have thought being homeless is much to celebrate,' she sighed.

He grinned as he followed her into the kitchen. 'You make me sound like a government statistic.'

She smiled, setting the bottle down carefully. 'Well . . . I'll just serve — '

'No hurry.' He came up behind her as she stirred the sauce. 'Mmm. Smells incredible.'

'It's a sweet and sour — ' she began.

'You, I mean.'

She felt him looking over her shoulder. 'Luke — '

'I know, I know,' he whispered in her ear. 'Don't fool around while you're cooking.'

'Or any other time,' she grumbled, nervously pouring the sauce into a small bowl. 'You're here to eat.'

'But both your hands are full.' He slid his arms around her waist, his breath teasing her neck.

'Luke, for goodness' sake . . . ' She let go of the saucepan, almost dropping the spoon. 'Luke!'

'I haven't done a thing,' he protested as she spun around, holding his hands in the air.

Her mistake was in moving too

swiftly out of his range. Her elbow clipped the long-necked bottle of wine and sent it orbiting around the table like a spinning top.

The explosion was deafening as it hit the floor. 'Oh, God,' she groaned, her hands going up to her mouth.

The frothy liquid ran up to the edges of her leather mules and to the tips of Luke's brown moccasins.

He caught her wrist as she bent. 'Don't,' he forbade her with a wry grin. 'You carry on with the food, I'll clear it up. Just point me in the direction of the mop.'

'But all that lovely wine . . . how could I have been so clusmy?' she bleated.

He gave her back her hand, kissing the back of it and looking up at her with mocking blue eyes. 'My innocent little cuddle was the problem. I'm sorry.'

Sophie despairingly showed him the utility-room and then returned to the hotplate, feeling wretched. She wished most of all that her hands would stop shaking just until she had served the meal, wishing, above all, the evening over.

'All clear,' she heard ten minutes later as Luke removed the artillery of cleaning equipment. He'd worn fawn cotton trousers and luckily they hadn't been spattered, but her eyes took their time to linger over the material and the way it hung perfectly on his long, muscular legs.

They collided at the door as she tried to exit and Luke searched for rogue splinters on the floor. He saved her as she almost toppled over him. Carefully he stood her upright with his big hands. 'I think we'd better eat. Next we'll have you fainting from hunger.'

She nodded, wishing she could crawl into a cupboard and stay there.

He tipped up her chin. 'Don't look so depressed — it was just a bottle of wine.'

She almost jumped at the touch of his fingers on her skin, but she managed to smile. 'To be perfectly honest,' she admitted on a sigh, 'I'm terribly nervous. It's just . . . I haven't done this sort of thing for a long while.'

'You haven't done anything — yet,' he grinned wickedly.

She snorted. 'You know what I mean!'

He smiled as his fingers stroked her neck, their tips causing little ripples of sensation to follow in their path. 'What am I going to do with you?' he sighed.

'Eat my food — I hope,' she answered, pushing away from him, heading warily back to the disaster area.

Ten minutes later they did eat, her eyes studying the neat white fingernails on long brown fingers as they moved sensuously over the food.

'Delicious.' He licked his lips hungrily. 'Is there pudding?' he asked rudely.

'Cheesecake, my *pièce de résistance*,' she laughed as she cleared the remains of the stir-fry, but his blue eyes teasing her made her fumble and suddenly knives and forks were flying everywhere. As if it had a life of its own, the carafe of water keeled over in the midst of them.

Luke threw back his head and laughed uproariously.

'Don't!' she cried, cheeks scarlet. 'This isn't funny any more!'

He jumped to his feet, trying to wipe the smile from his face. 'It's only water . . . look, no damage done.' He turned the glass bottle upright, took the plates from her shaking hands and piled the cutlery back on them.

'Hey . . . ' he murmured as he turned to find her standing rigidly, surveying the devastation. 'I'm sorry. I shouldn't have laughed.' He slid his arms around her waist and drew her to him. 'You do need a cuddle, Mrs Shaw, and, whether you like it or not, you're going to have one.'

The feeling of being taken into his arms, of his strong body against her, was just too good to fight. She let her head drop onto his shoulder as he stroked her hair.

'I'm sorry too,' she mumbled.

For a moment he held her, his hand kneading the back of her head, his fingers drawing slowly over her scalp. She made a small, unmeant sound of protest as he cupped her head between his large hands and looked into her face. Then, as she knew he would, he kissed her on the mouth, his fingers working the clips from her hair, allowing the blonde silk to fall through his fingers. When he had stopped kissing her her cheeks were flushed and her eyes a deep, rich brown.

'Leave all this,' he whispered. 'Let's find some neutral territory.'

He led her away from the table and she went willingly, his kiss still burning her mouth.

'This will have to do,' he said as he steered her into the drawing-room. Taking her shoulders, he pressed her down onto the sofa. 'You're a mess of nerves!' he told her, grinning. 'Do you promise to sit there and not move?'

She nodded, watching him go, struggling with the urge to rush after him and tell him she could cope, she was fine. But her legs felt like stones and her heart was palpitating so much that she was breathless.

Steamer padded in and sat beside her. With a sudden affection for the dog, she stroked his head, the comforting softness of his black fur beneath her fingers making her think of Luke's dark hair and the way it had felt when she had touched it, the night they danced, with her fingers linked at the back of his strong neck.

'Penny for your thoughts?' Luke walked in with two coffee mugs, lowering them to the glass coffee-table. Sitting beside her, he raised his eyebrows questioningly.

'You probably know them already,' she admitted.

'I know some of them — I think.'

'In the car . . . you said . . . I wanted everything to be perfect. I've been thinking — '

'That's your trouble,' he interrupted her gently. 'You think too much. Don't drive yourself too hard, or you'll become an expert at demolishing expensive bottles of wine.'

She sagged in her seat. 'I am sorry, truly.'

He slid an arm along the sofa. His fingers began to plunder her hair, removing the pins. 'Don't be sorry, be happy, my sweet.' He took her into his arms and kissed her again, her hands going up to find the hard jut of his shoulders as his lips searched hers, his tongue coming out to take possession of her mouth.

'Luke,' she protested weakly, but his lips silenced her protest, finding their way over her mouth again with hungry urgency. A low moan of excitement escaped her as his hand slipped seductively under her silk blouse to caress the soft skin of her back. It slid to the front and cupped her full breast, his fingers roving over the hardening bud beneath.

Too late she felt his own arousal as he leaned her back, beginning to unbutton the small pearls with a swift and urgent need. 'You're so lovely,' he whispered as she no longer resisted, aware her blouse was open and he had slipped the fastening of her bra.

'Luke . . . ' she murmured uselessly, arching her neck as he kissed her, his head going down to kiss the full white mounds he held in his hands.

'So beautiful . . . like soft creamy moons,' she heard him sigh. Her hands buried their way into his thick hair, sensation overwhelming her as he kissed and caressed her repeatedly, her need for him growing stronger with each sweet stroke of his tongue.

'Sophie, I want you,' he muttered as she found herself lying full length on the sofa, her head on the soft pillows, her cheeks flushed with desire.

She watched, fascinated, as the heavy-lidded blue eyes searched her own. She wanted him too, suddenly and too much. She fought the chemistry building inside her, her hands pushing against his chest. 'No, Luke . . . '

For a moment he waited, a small frown crossing his forehead. 'But you want this, Sophie, as much as I do. Listen to your body.'

'No. I don't know what I want — ' She felt a shiver going over her and she stiffened, feeling a mixture of shame and confusion for having allowed this to go so far.

He lifted himself, leaning on one elbow, studying her face, stroking his knuckle down her cheek. Her hands fumbled for her blouse as his fingers gently closed over them, helping her with the buttons.

'I . . . I'm — ' she began in a fluster. She saw his eyes soften as he looked at her, tenderness and understanding in them, and for a moment she hesitated.

He read her thoughts. 'It's either yes — or no, Sophie.'

'I didn't intend to . . . ' she began helplessly.

He frowned, tilting his head. 'Yes or

no. Simple decision.'

She finished buttoning up the rest of her blouse, her cheeks flushed in embarrassment. 'I feel so silly,' she whispered huskily.

'Feel free to feel anything you want,' he told her, then stayed her hand. Leaning across, he kissed her lightly.

'That's just a goodnight kiss,' he whispered. His voice was soft and she ached suddenly to be in his arms again.

'I'd better go,' he sighed with a rueful grin. 'I can't be responsible for my actions, little one, if I stay any longer.'

He hauled himself to his feet, reaching down for her hands. She took hold of them and he pulled her to her feet.

'I'm sorry we only had half a dinner,' she muttered as she slid a glance up at him.

He raised an eyebrow. 'The cheese-cake! I'd forgotten. Does that mean I might get a second invitation some time?' Giving her no chance to reply, he kissed her again. 'Walk me to the door and kick me out before I change my mind about going quietly.'

Somehow, managing to disengage herself and finding her way to the front door, she opened it. The cool evening air blew in and, drawing a lingering finger down her bare arm, he hesitated, but finally, reluctantly, he stepped out into the warm spring night.

★　★　★

Reality dawned the next morning as Ted Frost's wife called to say her husband had come down with a cold and that he would be delayed.

'Does that mean I get another meal this evening?' Luke asked when Sophie mustered enough courage to walk into his consulting-room and tell him.

She hesitated, hot colour burning her cheeks. 'I thought about ringing another builder — '

'Are you so desperate to get a roof over my head?' He shrugged. 'I slept like a log last night at the Cranthorpe if it makes you feel any better. How did you sleep?'

'Perfectly well.'

'Oh.' He pouted. 'I was hoping you didn't.'

'Luke, what happened last night — '

'Was delicious. Both the food and the company.'

She sighed. 'You know what I'm trying to say. We . . . you . . . us, it just won't work. Oh, heavens, don't just stand there looking at me like that.'

His eyes devoured her. 'I like looking at you. What else do you suggest I do when I talk to you? Look out of the window?'

She avoided his heavy-lidded gaze, mumbling something under her breath as she left, her heart quickening as she hurried to her room.

In her office she tried to forget last night, to forget everything that had happened since she'd known Luke, and to slip back into her routine.

She managed, for the rest of the day. Surprising herself, she coped for several days more, keeping calm when Ted still didn't appear to look at the bungalow. Keeping her distance from Luke posed less of a problem than she had anticipated, too, since when confronted with her presence he pointedly looked out of the nearest window with amused blue eyes.

★ ★ ★

The folllowing week she was working in her office when Jane tapped on the door. 'Patricia De Vere's arrived.' She giggled under her breath. 'Supposed to be an actress, would you believe? She wrapped her arms around Luke like an octopus when I showed her in.'

Sophie raised an eyebrow, sighing. 'I don't suppose Luke put up much of a fight,' she muttered under her breath.

'Oh, he always manages to joke his way out of things.' Jane paused reflectively. 'He's nice, isn't he? Never takes much seriously, yet he's such a brilliant vet. No wonder women fall

111

over themselves for him.'

'I hadn't noticed,' Sophie shrugged, an annoying little pain at her ribs when she thought of Patricia's elegant arms slipping adhesively around Luke's neck.

'Sophie, for heaven's sake snap out of it!' she muttered, angry with herself.

'They say the first sign of madness is talking to yourself,' a deep voice said.

She jerked up her head to find Luke grinning at her. 'The second is finding hairs on the palms of your hands.' He strolled in, reaching down to take hold of her hands, turning them palms upwards. 'Nope. Clean as a whistle. Completely uncertifiable.'

She tugged them irritably away. 'What do you want, Luke?'

'Just passing. You looked lonely.'

'I'm not — ' she began, only to stop as a second figure entered the office.

Patricia De Vere slid a long, slender arm through Luke's. 'We've already met, haven't we, Sophie?' she crooned in a silky smooth voice. Apparently not expecting an answer, she went on,

'Luke tells me he is staying in Cranthorpe, in a pub of all places! I've tried to persuade him to come and stay with us at Longhaven but he flatly refuses.'

'Too many actors cluttering up the place,' Luke protested amiably.

'It's an open house for the profession while we are resting,' Patricia stressed. She glanced at a sparkling gold band on her wrist. 'Is that really the time? Luke, may I have Maroc? I really must fly.'

Sophie watched — or rather heard — the departure of the actress and her borzoi.

'Quite something, isn't she?' Luke murmured as he sauntered back past her door. 'Bit of a chequered history, as it happens. Marriage to a famous producer, several notorious flings and a huge settlement from her divorce.'

'How interesting.' Sophie attacked her paperwork. Looking up to his amused grin, she demanded, 'No Ted Frost yet, I suppose?'

'Not yet. I rang him again today. Says

he'll be along as soon as he feels better.'
He looked under his long lashes at her.
'Does this delay mean I'm due another
dinner invitation?'

She smiled sweetly. 'I'm over my
guilty conscience. You're looking
incredibly healthy on pub food.'

'I'm not. I'm withering away!'

Luke's false protest did nothing to
dampen Sophie's admiration as she
helped him in Theatre the following
day. A mastiff called Hector lay
anaesthetised as Luke lifted the floppy
jowls for inspection. 'Hector has deep
periodontal pockets here on the distal
roots of these teeth. Monsters, aren't
they?'

Sophie shuddered as she wove the
aspirator over the pulpy area. 'He must
have been in terrible pain, poor animal.'

Luke flipped on the high-speed drill.
Controlled by his firm fingers, it
sectioned the first tooth at the bottom
nearest the gum, working up to the
biting surface.

She passed the elevator as he

systematically broke down the peri-odontal ligament, delicately placing the instrument between the two halves of the diseased tooth and easing it away. Finally, taking the forceps, he rotated and elevated the offending tooth from its socket.

This process repeated all over again on the neighbouring tooth, Sophie handed him the curettes. He used the spoon-shaped tool to scrape the inter-nal surface of the cavities, and when they were cleared and empty he nodded in satisfaction.

The gingiva or gum firmly sutured together, he pulled down his mask. 'Wash away, my sweet!' The broad white smile did nothing to help her keep her professional equilibrium as he waved Hector's dissected teeth, capped securely in a specimen bottle, in front of her. 'Souvenir of our first dental op together.'

'You're not really going to keep them?'

'I might even put them under my

pillow and see if the tooth fairy grants my wish,' he whispered provocatively in her ear.

'It's Hector's tooth — not yours,' she reminded him, moving swiftly out of range. 'Tooth fairies don't collect periodontal rejects.'

'Always worth the try.'

'Idiot,' she giggled.

Later, when Hector was dispatched, Luke brought his abundant notes to her with a smug smile. 'All entered. Hector's doing OK. I'll stay with him till he's round and then have Jane or Imelda check him at hourly intervals tonight.'

'Tell me, do you foresee any problems with Hector?' she asked in a businesslike tone, ignoring the way he was looking at her.

He slid into a chair. She made a great fuss of rechecking his notes, unable to look into the mesmeric blue gaze which was fixed, apparently, on her mouth.

'Certainly hope not. The bacteria destroyed some of the gum — apart from the periodontal ligament and the alveolar bone. It was exuding pus where the calculus and plaque had accumulated . . . he's going to feel sorry for himself for a couple of days. But that's all.'

Sophie nodded. 'Fine, then; I'll ring his owners.'

'When can I see you again, Sophie?' he asked quietly.

Forced to look up, she shrugged. 'We see each other every day.'

He growled. 'Don't be evasive.'

'Luke, if you mean the other night — '

'I mean I want to see you again, away from work. Tonight preferably.'

'No.'

'Why not?'

'You're on call, or have you forgotten?' she reminded him sharply.

'Is that a refusal?'

'Point blank.'

He watched her lower her eyes. 'You're working too hard. You need to relax.'

Her lids flew up. 'I can and do relax, when I want to.'

'With your friend Hamish Burns, I suppose?' he muttered moodily.

'Hamish? What do you mean?' she demanded as her heart skipped a beat.

'I mean . . . you must have a little fun with someone?'

'And your ego won't allow you to believe it's not with you?' she asked angrily.

He nodded. 'Close enough.'

She thrust him back the notes. 'Hamish, if you must know, is an old friend. We've known each other for years.' She ignored his disbelieving look. 'Just like you and your friend the actress!' she added spitefully.

'Ah ha!' He made a face. 'Now I understand.'

She opened her mouth and then shut it. Jumping to her feet, she grabbed the paperwork in front of her, pulled it to her pounding breast and left the office with an expressive snort of disgust.

5

The following day, Thursday, Sophie decided to shop in Cranthorpe during her lunch-hour. On her return she discovered Ted Frost by the bungalow, down on his knees, peering into a hole he'd dug below the damp course.

'It looks like subsidence,' he muttered grimly. 'There's a problem in the foundations as well as inside. Could take a bit longer than we thought.'

Sophie asked warily, 'How long?'

Ted stood up and leaned on his spade. 'A month or two ... maybe more.'

The next half an hour was a blur. Basically, the place was a danger zone, she was told, needing reconstruction below ground level as well as in the lounge, which was, ironically, the least of her worries.

Afterwards Sophie collapsed in a

chair in her office.

'Bad news, isn't it?' Howard appeared, having received the verdict.

'Luke knows?'

He nodded. 'The insurance will cough up; I've been in touch with them and we're covered.'

Sophie nodded. 'But what about Luke?'

Howard looked at her with concern. 'Luke can come to us. He's thinking about buying soon, anyway.'

'But Molly has the grandchildren, Howard,' Sophie protested.

'We just won't have them so regularly.' He shrugged. 'No problem.'

'But it wouldn't be fair on Molly.' She shook her head. Her lips moved though she could hear no sound coming out as her heart hurled itself from one side of her chest to the other. 'He can come to me, Howard.' She gazed up at the older man's surprised expression. She even managed to laugh. 'The company will probably do me good.'

* * *

Imelda called from the passageway, 'Hamish is on the line, Sophie. Shall I switch it through to your office?'

Sophie hesitated, then with a sigh shouted, 'Yes, I'll take it, Imelda; transfer the call, please.'

'Time enough for some things, then?' Luke called in a sardonic tone as he passed by the office.

She waved him away, picking up the phone. 'Hamish?'

'How about our evening out?' she heard and, trying to think quickly, hovered between an excuse and the truth.

'Soon, Hamish,' she compromised. After putting down the phone, she glanced up, her eyes locking into crisp blue ones. 'That was supposed to be a private call, you know.'

Luke shrugged, walking in. 'Didn't hear a word.'

Her colour deepened. 'You saw Ted Frost, I gather?'

'I did.' He lounged against a wall, long arms folded.

'You can take that smile off your face,' she muttered, knowing exactly what he was thinking.

'A little more than we bargained for,' he observed unnecessarily.

'You're looking for a house in Cranthorpe, Howard says?' she asked in hope.

'Ah . . . but I'm particular.'

She sighed and leaned back. 'Of that I have no doubt. Meanwhile . . . '

'Meanwhile, I wouldn't dream of imposing,' he lied badly.

'Well . . . ' Her heart gave a little flutter. 'I suppose you'd better use my guest room until you've found a house.' There, she'd said it. Her only chance was, by some miracle, he'd refuse.

He didn't. 'Great — when?' he asked immediately, sticking out his wrist and examining his watch.

'Not now!' Sophie jumped to her feet. 'Luke . . . ' she hesitated, suddenly developing serious cold feet ' . . . I don't know . . . I'm not sure . . . '

He lifted broad shoulders. 'Ground rules — we need some ground rules, yes?'

Surprised, she nodded.

He shrugged, ambling to the door, turning to look at her with wide, innocent eyes. 'You make them, I'll abide by them. I promise I'm going to be an exemplary guest. Er — when can you fit me in?'

Repressing a smile, she relented. 'Tomorrow, I suppose.'

She was still uncertainly considering what she had done when, at six, she turned to the window and gazed out on an immaculate evening. At the same time she saw Luke's tall figure stride casually across to the car park towards a shiny little red sports car. As Luke bent down to talk to her the female driver threw back her dark head and laughed.

Sophie saw the lovely young woman was Amanda Drew.

★ ★ ★

The next morning Luke accompanied Howard on his farm visits, and Sophie breathed a sigh of relief at the prospect of the few hours' respite.

John was in open surgery during the morning assisted by Jane, allowing Sophie time to catch up on her computer work. She was not surprised when Howard rang in to say that they would be delayed. The senior partner was ever inclined to participate in the farmers' hospitality when offered and the introduction of a new member of staff, it appeared, was cause for such an indulgence.

John took his appointments in the afternoon and it was four o'clock by the time Howard and Luke returned. Sophie could see the farm visits had gone well enough by Howard's flushed face, his eyes bright as he and Luke talked in the corridor.

'All's well?' Howard asked positively as they entered the office.

Sophie nodded, aware of Luke's tall form sauntering in, reminding her again of a dozen horrifying scenarios which could take place in the first hour of having Luke under her roof.

Howard smiled indulgently. 'This man smeared washing-up liquid all over Chas Bell's sow, who had her head stuck in between iron bars. Got her on her side, doused her with the stuff and pulled like a Christmas cracker. Came out beautifully, blowing bubbles.'

Sophie's eyebrows lifted sardonically. 'How fortunate for Chas Bell's sow.'

'And Luke's going to take out some freezer-branding equipment for Pete Arnott's cows. Pete's been wanting to have a look at the apparatus, but never got round to it.'

'Lucky for Pete,' Sophie murmured, irritably aware that Howard was impressed.

'Well, I'm off to brew a strong cup of tea,' Howard sighed, bewildered at having stirred no interest in his female listener. 'That barley wine of Pete's has given me a thirst. I'll see you two in a minute.'

He disappeared and Sophie found

her eyes locked with Luke's.

'What have I done?' he asked. 'I'll turn to stone if you keep looking at me like that.'

'Nothing,' she snapped. What did it matter to her if Luke had a dozen women calling to see him in little red sports cars, just as long as it didn't interfere with his work?

Luke laughed aloud. 'You're worried what people will say, aren't you, about us — our living together?'

She shot him a killing look. 'We are not living together — not cohabiting — not sharing anything except perhaps the kitchen.'

'Ground rules,' he said soberly. 'I understand.'

'I suppose you can cook?'

'I can boil a perfect egg.'

'Good. As long as you can look after yourself.'

He handed her the diary for which she was searching. 'In other words, you want me self-sufficient?'

'It would help.' She opened the book,

her eyes blindly reviewing the page. 'You've had plenty of practice, I'm sure, in between . . . friends.'

His face crumpled. 'Ouch! A bit below the belt, that one, my sweet.'

'The truth always hurts, apparently. And I'm not your sweet.'

'But you are grumpy.'

'I am not grumpy either!' She gave up looking at the blurred page. 'I'm just busy.'

He grinned. 'So am I, but I'd much rather be in here talking to you, even though you are grumpy.'

'Out!' she spat and watched him leap from the office.

Water off a duck's back, she thought, and, shaking her head at the dreadful metaphor he provoked, picked up a pen, knowing she wasn't going to concentrate on a thing.

★ ★ ★

Up at the crack of dawn on Saturday, Sophie set about the guest room.

It was a spacious, modern bedroom, facing south, brimming with light and sun. She had a sudden, piercing vision of Luke's long body in the wide double bed as she made it up with fresh cotton sheets.

Was she not mad? she asked herself for the hundredth time as she closed her eyes and drew her hand across her damp brow.

The doorbell rang too early, before she had changed from her shorts and T-shirt.

'Sorry about the time,' Luke apologised, not looking sorry at all, but staring at her long, uncovered legs ending in a pair of flimsy flipflops. 'They wanted my room, you see. Sudden influx of visitors. Do you mind?'

When the freefalling of her heart stopped, luckily before it hit her stomach, she nodded, opening the door wider. He looked taller and larger than ever, dressed in thigh-hugging blue jeans and a blue and white checked shirt open at the neck, cuffs turned back over brown forearms.

'Come in,' she mumbled ungraciously.

'Two suitcases.' Luke jerked his head to the path behind him. 'Shall I dispose of them first?'

She eyed the fat-looking luggage with a sinking feeling.

'Hmm!' Luke exclaimed admiringly as she showed him the room and he stacked the cases side by side at the foot of the bed. 'Bathroom?' he asked.

She led the way, pushing open the door.

'Very chic. And — er — your room?'

She waved her hand in the general direction. 'I'll leave you to unpack,' she called over her shoulder as she hurried downstairs.

In the kitchen, she dragged in a breath, busying herself with preparing the coffee, wishing she had at least had time to put on a dress. Long legs had always been a source of concern for her, buying the right length trousers and wearing hemlines which looked their best either well above or below the knee. Shorts, therefore, were pure luxury, especially the denim ones she wore today, revealing enough thigh and calf unfortunately to make her feel self-conscious in her visitor's presence.

Considering whether she should rush upstairs and change them, she turned impetuously to collide with a broad chest just entering the kitchen.

'Oh, sorry!' She sprang back clumsily.

He grinned. 'Making your escape?'

She turned back to the coffee, even more aware of the penetrating gaze.

'Coffee smells good!' Taking a mug from her, he glanced around with a wry smile. 'Funny how familiar this room seems already.'

Ignoring this, she slid open a drawer. 'Er — frontdoor key. Labelled, of course, so you won't get it mixed up with the others. As for meals — '

He dropped it into his shirt pocket. 'I promise I won't get under your feet.

130

One advantage of a bachelor life is learning that if you don't clear away after you, nobody else does.'

She hesitated. 'Luke, I think there is something . . . '

'Ground rules,' he provided bluntly.

'Well . . . yes.'

'I've promised to behave myself.' He leaned against the worktop, looking lean, honed and well muscled, the enjoyment on his face evident at her unease. 'Mind you, there may be occasions when you'll have to keep me in order. Full moon, high tide, et cetera.'

'Luke, I — '

'Did anyone ever tell you you look very sexy in shortie shorts?'

'I . . . I didn't have time to change.'

His mouth curled up in a lazy smile. 'All the better to see you with.'

'Don't you ever give up?' she bleated, pulling in a mouthful of air, pink streaks appearing on her face.

He shrugged. 'I have this curious feeling you don't want me to. The way your lovely body kind of talks, expresses itself — it's almost as though it was saying the opposite to what I hear.'

'That's ridiculous.' Panic began to set in as the phone rang.

'I'll go. My Saturday for being on call,' he sighed, putting down his coffee and heading out to the hall.

Having Luke as a house guest was, she decided, worse than she had thought. She was as nervous as a kitten — and had little hope of feeling better while he was following her about the house.

'Want to come with me?' he asked on his return. 'Can I tempt you to a nice case of foot rot on a little pony at Chas Bell's farm?'

She grinned. 'Too exciting for me, thanks all the same.'

He looked at her with dismay. 'Party pooper.'

When he had finally gone, she put a hand on her heart. Amazed it was still in the same place, she realised with some bewilderment that the day now stretched safely ahead of her since her major problem had been removed and she was at liberty to do exactly as she pleased.

* * *

John Marks rang the next morning at eight to say he had caught a viral infection and was going back to bed in the hopes that he could sweat it out for Monday.

Sophie listened to the unusual noises in the house as she put the phone down. Running water and whistling came from the bathroom upstairs interspersed with the opening and closing of doors.

Luke eventually came downstairs, his freshly showered, lean body dressed in cool white cotton trousers and a navy blue shirt.

'I hope I didn't disturb you when I came in last night?' he asked as he followed her into the dining-room, where she had set breakfast.

'No, not at all.'

He rubbed his hands together. 'Do we eat like this every morning?'

She served eggs and bacon from a dish, placing the plate in front of him. 'I wanted to talk to you and the safest place seemed to be here, with table and food dividing us.'

'Fire away.'

She hesitated, watching him wield the knife and fork. 'Luke, I feel we should . . . '

He ate ravenously, the wide mouth absorbing food and coffee with breathtaking efficiency. 'May I have more toast?'

She pushed forward the rack. 'As I was saying — '

'This is brilliant,' he crunched. He stretched out his hand towards yet another slice. 'May I?'

She nodded. 'Luke . . . you make me feel — '

'Aren't you eating?' he asked, staring at her untouched plate.

'I'm trying to talk to you!' she

exclaimed in despair.

He lowered his knife and fork, eyebrows raised.

'I just feel . . . threatened, somehow.'

'As if I'm invading your space?' he provided helpfully, demolishing the last of the bacon.

'Well . . . in a way, yes, but — '

'I promise — ' he raised his right hand solemnly ' — not to lay a finger on you while I'm your guest — not even one small cuddle. How's that?'

'You promise?'

'I promise.'

She blushed, supposing she would have to be content with this tenuous agreement, but she could hardly endure many more nights like last night, wondering every second when he was going to appear.

As he ate she found herself gazing at the brown hair-strewn arms under the turned-back cuffs, the wet black hair slicked into place over his well-shaped head, the hunch of broad shoulders beneath the blue shirt.

'How was your foot rot?' she asked, dragging her eyes away, dipping her knife into the butter, mentally calculating that the diagnosis and treatment would not have accounted for the length of his evening-long absence.

'Fine,' he told her vaguely. 'I had another call afterwards, a Caesar in Cranthorpe, a little spaniel bitch. Two alive — one dead pup, blocking the escape hatch. Then I called in to see a friend on my way home. You didn't wait up for me, by any chance, did you?'

'I certainly did not.' She had lost her appetite. What friend? she wondered.

His plate cleared, he sat back with a sigh, eyes lifting to the ceiling, where they remained as he murmured, 'Ground rules, ah . . . yes.'

Her eyes flew wide open. 'And what's that supposed to mean?'

'Oh, nothing.' He met her suspicious gaze. 'Funny thing, chemical attraction. It's like lightning. Strikes suddenly and without warning — '

'Don't tease, Luke! This is important to me.'

'Important I don't seduce you, you mean. Or at least try to. Which I'm not. Be honest with me, Sophie.' He leaned forward, his eyes a deep, seductive blue. 'Aren't you just in the least little bit tempted?'

'You promised!' she groaned, pushing back her chair.

'I promised — like a fool.' He grinned. 'Despite the fact that I find you incredibly attractive and I just happen to be enjoying your company too.'

She stood up. He stretched out a long arm and held her wrist as she went to walk away, the pads of his fingers burning on her skin. 'Friends?' he asked softly.

★　★　★

Much to everyone's surprise, John's virus incapacitated its victim for a full week. Sophie found herself one vet and one nurse short as the days lengthened and an outbreak of summer mastitis among the dairy herds kept Luke permanently out on visits.

Howard split surgeries with the only other vet in Cranthorpe, Percy Deer, and the night-time coverage was shouldered, in the main, by Luke.

On Sunday morning, the first in June, Sophie woke muzzily to the intrusive noise of the telephone, managing to focus her gaze on the clock's luminous hands, pointing at five past five.

'Mum, is that you?' she asked sleepily.

'Hannah's in labour,' her mother told her anxiously, 'and straining badly. Can you come?'

'I'll be right over with a vet,' Sophie mumbled, shrugging, as she spoke, out of her nightie. In less than ten minutes she was dressed in jeans and a cool cotton shirt, wondering just how bad her father's part-Arab mare was. Hannah was beautiful, cream coated

138

and long legged, but motherhood had eluded her once before and Michael had warned against another pregnancy.

As Luke was the vet on call, she knocked twice on his door. With no reply, she realised he must have been called out during the night. Her mind raced over the alternatives; Howard or Percy Deer. Howard would have to come in from town, Percy from even further away.

Left with little choice but to trouble Howard and with her hand on the telephone, she saw the front door open. Luke's tired, yawning face appeared as he managed a grin. 'Up already?' he frowned, small lines of tiredness running from the corners of his eyes.

'You look all in,' she sighed, realising he was probably exhausted. The mastitis outbreak had come at the very worst time.

'Trouble?' he persisted, frowning down at the telephone in her hand.

Reluctantly, she explained. The tiredness left his eyes as he told her to jump in the Jaguar while he collected the necessary medication for parturition from the practice. Minutes later they were speeding through Cranthorpe towards Collingwood Farm.

As they drove she explained how six-year-old Hannah had lost her foal three years ago. Michael had warned her father not to put her to stud again unless he was prepared to face difficulties.

'And Howard has seen her through this pregnancy?'

Sophie shrugged. 'Yes, twice. Dad hasn't had any problems so far. He thought everything was going to be all right.'

'It probably will be,' Luke told her. But somehow Sophie wasn't so sure. Michael had been good with horses — he wouldn't have given the warning to her father for nothing. And now she wondered why her father had gambled again.

Anne Edmonds was waiting for them. Sophie made swift introductions and her mother led them through the house and into the cobbled yard, towards the line of modern, well-kept stables.

Inside Hannah's box, the overhead light glimmered dully. Sophie was dismayed to see her father's anxious face. Ralph Edmonds, a tall, burly man with a head of silver-grey hair, was sponging off his horse, his shirt bathed in sweat.

'Michael delivered her first, a still-born,' he said without preamble, nodding at Luke. 'I expect Sophie told you.'

Luke stripped off his sweater, leaving his torso naked, in order to examine the horse without hindrance. The mare's stomach and distended vulva took only a few minutes to assess, and his forehead furrowed in concern.

'How is it lying?' her father asked impatiently.

Luke thrust his arms into the hot water provided. Some of it splashed onto him, drawing Sophie's attention from Hannah to the forest of black hair that grew thickly across Luke's tightly muscled chest.

'The foal has its front legs and body pointing upwards,' he explained, 'and as she becomes recumbent there's always the chance she might drive the forelimbs into the roof of the vagina.'

'What about the head?' her father asked, looking even more worried. 'The last foal was asphyxiated. Can't we help her to move it out quicker?'

'So far, the head's safe,' Luke assured him calmly. 'Speeding the delivery is as dangerous as no assistance at all. I'm going to try to slide its feet along and prevent them from penetrating into the rectum.'

Sophie helped her mother replenish with fresh water and towels. She knew that if a fistula or opening between rectum and vagina happened when Hannah sank to the ground to give birth, the little feet would be trapped and the rest of the body prevented from emerging. She also knew, as did her

142

parents, that in trying to correct the problem there was a risk to Hannah's life, as, indeed, to the life of her offspring. Nature's way was not meant to be interfered with and the skilled manoeuvres to help it along were best learned by practice and only acquired by people with great professional skill and experience.

She watched anxiously as, reaching inside Hannah again, Luke began to try to ease the miniature feet with their soft covering of horn over the vagina roof. In the effort, his forehead beaded with sweat and she took a sponge to wipe it away from his eyes. Pain was etched across his face as his arm became trapped in a muscular contraction.

'Steady her,' he called gruffly to Ralph Edmonds as the horse began its descent to the floor.

'Stay with it, lad,' her father muttered, catching hold of the head-collar and doing his best to control Hannah's thrashing head.

143

Luke arched his glistening back with a grunt, going with the movement of the horse. With the next contraction it seemed he had managed to shift the hooves to safety as tiny nose, head and foetal chest all appeared safety. Sophie saw he was using all his strength to prevent the umbilical cord from being squashed on the floor of Hannah's pelvis.

It was at this point, she reflected, that the mare's last delivery had gone wrong. The foal's umbilical cord had been squeezed and its source of oxygen from the placenta shut off.

Hannah let out a groan. With his head against her straining body, Luke's hand skilfully stimulated the natural arc of delivery inside and, to the relief of everyone, Hannah's beautiful newborn suddenly lay in the straw.

'How is he?' her father asked anxiously, watching Luke clear the foal's mouth and throat in order that he might breathe.

Luke grinned as the struggling first

movements spoke for themselves and Hannah, delighted, whinnied her welcome.

The delivery over, Sophie had an overwhelming desire to rush to Luke and throw her arms around him. He turned to smile at her and their eyes met, sending hot colour blazing to her cheeks at his discovery of her hungry gaze.

'Just the placenta to come,' he said quietly, and Sophie watched as the two men moved back to allow Hannah to handle the completion of her parturition in privacy.

'Where's your mother?' Ralph Edmonds whispered as he joined her at the back of the box.

'I don't think she could bear the suspense,' Sophie grinned as her father slid an arm around her shoulders.

He chuckled and gave her a wink. 'We'll finish up here. How about some breakfast and coffee in the house?'

Sophie caught Luke's smile at the mention of breakfast and mentally totalled up the number of eggs that would be needed to satisfy this ravenous man's appetite.

★　★　★

It became a celebratory meal, as both her parents had waited for Hannah's foal in trepidation for eleven long months. Luke sensed the occasion and treated her parents to the sharpest of his wit.

He hadn't slept a wink for hours but still he was able to joke. He grinned at Sophie across the table, showing no signs of the exhaustion that must certainly grind at his limbs.

'What made you want to settle in Cranthorpe?' Anne Edmonds asked, and Sophie was suddenly uncomfortably aware that, now the crisis of Hannah was over, another had arisen — her mother's curiosity!

Luke met Sophie's eyes briefly. 'Kent was where I was born, Mrs Edmonds,' he responded politely, 'and always

146

seemed like home.'

'I — er — think it's time we should be going,' Sophie interrupted, aware of the sudden undertones of the conversation. 'Luke is still on call, Mum.'

'Just until lunchtime,' he grinned, stretching.

Sophie tore her rebellious eyes away from the broad chest rising as he expelled a long, slow breath.

'I'm sorry about the interrogation,' Sophie apologised when they finally made their escape and were at last seated in the Jaguar. She drew her small hands over her aching brow. 'Mum means well enough, but I'm still twelve in her eyes. My brothers have moved from Cranthorpe with their families . . . she only has me to worry about and I'm afraid she does that rather well.'

'They're nice people,' he said quietly. 'You're lucky.'

Sophie nodded, aware that she was — incredibly lucky. As they drove she considered what it must be like to grow up without the love and security of a close family. Luke had had neither of these things.

It was odd, but she felt she understood a little more of him each day. His bond with Louise and Phillipa and Martin, of whom he constantly talked, had replaced his familial bond with his parents. His opinion of marriage was reflective of his bachelor status and his attitude to women. At least she had ten years of loving Michael and could grieve for love lost. But Luke had not loved, at least not enough to marry. He would not let himself love.

'You must be very tired,' she said softly.

'Hmm. Bed does have its attraction.' He looked over at her, his face wry. 'Want to tuck me in?'

She laughed, her laughter springing from a deep sense of relief that the trauma of Hannah and her foal was over and the secret pleasure she felt in going home to share her house with a man who was rapidly becoming a part of her life.

He smiled smugly. 'I knew I was winning you over.'

6

'I'll ring Howard and confirm the change-over,' Sophie said as they pulled up at the house. 'Then I'll unplug the phone in the hall so it won't disturb you while you crash out for a few hours.'

'Trying to get rid of me?' Luke asked as they walked towards the house.

She grinned. 'After what you did today?' She shook her head. 'No, you're too valuable an asset to the practice, I'm afraid.'

He snorted. 'That sounds suspiciously like flattery.'

She paused on the doorstep. It wasn't flattery, but praise. Had it not been for Luke, both Hannah and her foal could have died today.

He unlocked and pushed open the door as Steamer leapt out, barking. She watched his long arms tumble over the dog, roll him on his back and ruffle the squirming chest. 'Good lad, let's nip in the garden for a bit, shall we?' He looked up at her with a grin. 'Shan't be long. Call of nature.'

Sophie watched him walk into the garden with Steamer at his heels, his long tail beating furiously. Hands thrust in pockets, broad back upright and square, Luke looked as though he'd always fitted into the routine of the house and her heart suddenly jerked. How easily he had become a part of every day.

She was suddenly afraid.

Hurrying in, she put her mind to ringing Howard, then, when the transition was made and a few words pleasantly passed with Molly, Sophie unplugged the hall extension. This done, she went into the kitchen, made an unnecessary pot of tea and looked out of the kitchen window on to the back lawn.

It revealed only Steamer, who happily gnawed on an unearthed marrowbone, oblivious to the rest of the world. Luke, she decided, must have come in the front way and headed upstairs, perhaps to shower.

Leaving the tray, she walked into the hall to listen for revealing sounds. The house was in silence. Something made her turn to the drawing-room, though at first glance it looked empty.

As she walked in her eyes fell to the sofa and the figure lying on it. Luke's long body sprawled there, one long leg angled awkwardly on the cushions, foot dangling off the end. He was too big to fit on it properly and his sweater twisted around his broad chest, as though unconsciously he had wriggled down to squeeze himself into place.

Her mouth dried as she saw the brown gap of skin between jeans and top. A few black hairs curled provocatively across the taut skin, winking at her, promising her there were many more above, as she very well knew.

The hands she had watched today, so long-fingered and agile, lay limply, tips touching the floor, the other hand cast behind his head, reminding her of someone about to effect a hornpipe.

The thought made her smile. Observing him like this brought tenderness and desire mixed in her breast. She had a need to touch him, to see if he was real, to stroke the beautiful body which lay before her so innocently and, for once, devoid of lust.

Quietly kneeling beside him, she gazed at the long, thick black lashes. Even in sleep he gave the impression of sensuality, but it was harnessed and at bay, like a sleeping tiger's.

His skin was grainy, his nose straight; carved shadows under the eyes spoke of tiredness, yet with them closed, no blue pools to drown in, his face invited a different kind of emotion.

She studied every nook and cranny of the handsome face, the thick black hair, the heavy eyebrows, the voraciously full mouth.

Had she realised her lips were so close to his? Had he known she was studying him? Her heart almost went into shock as his hand slipped over her head and brought her mouth firmly down on his.

Desire sent her rushing down a path she had never trodden before. Her mouth opened obediently, his tongue entered and probed the sweetness of her mouth and her fleeting struggle was over as he crushed her to him, strong arms wrapping around her like some great bear as he gently half lifted, half slithered her from the floor, on top of him.

'You were staring at me,' he murmured lazily, his long legs opening to let her slim ones fall through. 'What were you looking for?'

She swallowed, unable to move in his arms. 'I was . . . going to say I'd made tea.'

The blue eyes twinkled. 'Really?'

She nodded.

He tilted his head. 'I don't believe you.'

'Well, it's tr — ' she began and then stopped because he was laughing.

She pushed up, palms hard against his chest, managing to lift her upper body. 'Don't tease — '

'I'm not.' He pressed her down again. 'Admit you were sitting there wishing you could seduce me.'

She glared at him. 'You're so arrogant!'

'No . . . in truth, I lack confidence.'

She gasped. 'Rubbish!'

He looked at her for a long while. 'Come to bed with me, Sophie.'

The swift, assured gesture and suggestion, for once, did not surprise her. His arousal was evident beneath her and her body responded equally through her clothes, tensing and shivering against him. She wanted to, so much. Her throbbing breasts ached to be caressed and a heat ebbed and flowed low in her stomach, marauding through her bones.

She bit her lip. 'You promised . . . '

'Sophie,' he whispered, his mouth smoothing against her cheek, 'I want you — and by the feel of your beautiful body I think you want me. Don't keep me to a promise neither of us wants me to keep?' He brushed a hand through her hair.

'I can't — '

'You can,' he corrected her huskily. 'You can do anything you want, Sophie. You aren't married any longer. You're not being disloyal . . . or having an affair. At some point you are going to have to admit you're a healthy, young, single woman who has a perfect right to satisfy her physical and emotional needs.'

He kissed her, slowly, tenderly, destroying the last of her defences, then he picked her up in his arms and began to carry her towards the stairs.

She was aware of every step, his fingers closed around her arms, her hands around his neck, the thrust of his body as he walked, the clamour of excitement that pulsed within her as they ascended the stairs. And the voice of reason calling softly within, Stop, before it's too late.

His grip tightened as they came to the landing and they passed his door.

'Not here, Luke,' she whispered as they entered her bedroom.

'Why not?' He lowered her to the big double bed. The bed she had slept in, made love in, woken in, with Michael.

'It just doesn't feel right . . . '

He laid her down, his blue eyes glimmering beneath their moist lids. 'We are going to exorcise those damn ghosts,' he muttered under his breath, his fingers brushing over the damp softness of her neck, running up into her tousled hair.

He bent to kiss her, the heat of his body penetrating the thin material of her T-shirt, crushing her down into the soft linen.

'No,' she begged again. It was inconceivable. This room was hers and Michael's. It would seem like sacrilege to make love to another man here.

'It's just a bed,' he whispered soothingly, brushing his thumbs against the peaking desire of her breasts, making her gasp, her hands dragging tensely up in protest.

As she moved he caught her wrists and bent to kiss each palm and the tiny blue veins above, activating the pounding throb of her heart in sudden pleasure.

'Trust me,' he whispered as he peeled her T-shirt up from her waist, drawing it over her head and slowly over each slim arm.

Her full breasts below the lacy white bra throbbed as he groaned, staring at them. 'You're beautiful, Sophie, so beautiful.' He unclipped the front fastening, his dark head going down to kiss and coax each tiny hardening bud with his tongue, his hands cupping their full beauty with gentle pressure.

'Oh, Luke,' she heard herself sigh as she closed her eyes, melting with the consuming need that burnt like a raging fire inside her body.

His hands trailed over her, discovering her as her mouth parted on a soft, welcoming moan of pleasure. Somehow her jeans were removed by a very capable pair of hands. She saw them vaguely drop to the floor.

'Come here,' he mouthed, disposing of the white boxer shorts over narrow hips and hard thighs making her gasp in hungry desire as he brought her to him and bent to caress her breasts, his tongue a slow and clever tease, bringing a gasp of shuddering pleasure from her lips.

'Hold me,' he whispered and she did as he bade her, her uncertain hands seeking to return the pleasure he was giving her. The electric intimacy of shared discovery pulsed between them as his mouth covered hers.

Too late to think, to care, she decided. Her need overpowered her, like some strange alien force which had taken over her body, driving it beyond the bounds of reason and far beyond that little voice inside.

His gaze lingered over her nakedness, her soft, feminine figure, her long legs entwined with his own darker ones, her gentle curve of hip and his harder, leaner body, his leg muscle indenting as he flexed, drawing her into his possession.

Neither two years of celibacy, nor the long and loyal years of marriage had revealed to her the hungry animal within her own breast. Released now, it thirsted for the satisfaction of long hours of aloneness. This man filled her need.

She knew it now. Stored up in her innermost self, her passion escaped its shackles as darts of flame shot through her, brown eyes smouldering as she begged, 'Make love to me, Luke,' the air clogging in her throat, her nails digging over his shoulders as he arched over her.

The brief pause in their need caused his dark eyebrows to rise. In a moment of understanding she realised she hadn't thought of protection, hadn't even considered the likelihood of needing it.

Hot colour flooded her cheeks.

'There?' she mumbled, her eyes going to the drawer, her heart almost stopping as he reached across her and slid it open.

Seconds later, his search successful, he returned to move against her, lifting her gently into his arms. 'I want you, Sophie. Don't hide your feelings. Give them their freedom,' he groaned, softly touching her eyes with his mouth. Then, leaving no curve of her face unkissed, he descended, dragging his lips slowly down until she writhed with pleasure at his exquisite torment, seeking and obtaining a response from every inch of her quivering skin.

At last she cupped his head and begged him to stop. He drew her under him as slowly he drove her to her limit, entering her on a shudder of desire that demanded, without question, her complete surrender.

She gave it, matching his energy, until at last, exhausted, they lay in breathless collapse, the breath locked in her throat as her body trembled into sleep in the circle of his arms.

★ ★ ★

The sun had drifted in an arc around the room. A few soft rays peeped in against the creamy white curtains, sending the shafts in delicate fingers to the bed.

Luke stirred beside her. She moved slowly, turning to see if she had dreamt him. But their lovemaking was no dream, she knew, as he moved and caused the same quivering reaction inside her that had sent her willingly into his arms.

The pale sheet across his brown body tugged at the black hairs of his chest, the chest which had lain across her and driven her to such heights of pleasure. She shivered as she thought of her uninhibited response as they had made love, wondering how she would meet his eyes when he opened them.

His soft, regular breathing rose and

fell under the linen. He moved again, one long arm stretching out as her heart raced. Was it, she wondered, to find her?

The blue eyes suddenly opened as if in answer, the thick lashes around them like tiny dark wings. Words locked in her throat as he reached out to draw her towards him.

'Come here, little one.' He pulled her down into the warmth of his arms, kissing the blush on her cheeks, amusement in his eyes as he eased her arms around him, encircled her legs with his own. 'What am I going to do with you? That brain of yours is working overtime again,' he whispered, one dark eyebrow lifting.

He kissed her, running his hand over the curve of her cheek, his caress tender. 'Are you angry with me for breaking my promise?'

She made herself meet his eyes. 'I . . . it wasn't you.'

He kissed her again, drawing her hair through his fingers. He tilted up her chin. 'I need you, Sophie, I want you. Let me convince you, let me make love to you again.' His fingers slid down the soft curve of her arm and drifted over the full, feminine thrust of her breast. Desire stabbed through her, wantonly, violently.

At this moment, she needed him too.

They left the bed only to allow Steamer his freedom in the garden. Their need to match and exhaust each other's energies as the night closed darkly around the house overcame even the need to eat.

In the shower they made love, slowly, deliciously in a torrent of lukewarm water. He dried her hair for her afterwards with a fluffy white towel, removing her silk robe, taking her back to bed with her body still damp.

Somewhere in the lost hours she fell asleep, her body curved around him under the sheet, her arm threaded under his, the smell of his hair in her nostrils as they drifted, satiated, in the hours before dawn.

She woke, finding herself alone. Only the indented pillow beside her and her sensitised body caused her to remember in a flood the events of the last twenty-four hours.

The house was silent as she slipped on her robe and hurried downstairs. The long case clock in the hall struck half-past eight and she gazed at it disbelievingly, unable to recall when she had slept in so late.

Steamer snuffled her as she entered the kitchen and there on the table she found a slip of notepaper, recognising Luke's spidery scrawl: 'Take your time, honey, don't rush in.'

Her mind fled to what the staff might think. She had never been late before. Wouldn't everyone guess what had happened? After all, Luke staying at the house was an open invitation . . .

Sophie managed to calm her chaotic thoughts. She showered and dressed in a cool cream linen suit and made the bed with clean sheets.

Had that really been her? Had she,

Sophie Shaw, made such wanton, seemingly endless love? Had she really given herself to a man so intimately, sleeping so soundly until she had belatedly woken from her exhausted surrender?

She walked into the surgery at nine-fifteen. The waiting-room, thankfully, was so crowded that she passed through unnoticed, the girls busy at the desk. All the consulting-room doors were closed, which meant the vets were in consultation.

Sophie hurried into the office and closed the door. Safe. Nothing disturbed. The mail piled on her desk neatly by Jane or Imelda. One of the girls had thought to switch on the percolator for her too.

Sophie sat at her desk and flicked her terminal, breathing a sigh of relief. The screen blinked back at her and automatically she slid in a disc. Concentrate, she told herself. Stop thinking. Work.

But, ten minutes later, the door

opened and wordlessly she met Luke's blue gaze.

'Busy?'

Sophie shook her head.

'Sleep well?' he whispered in a teasing voice.

Sophie shot a glance to the open door behind him. Going to it, she closed it gently. Before she had time to open her mouth he swung her around and into his arms and kissed her deeply. 'I needed that,' he grinned, kissing her chin and neck, making her legs turn to water.

'Luke, be careful,' she said softly, gently extricating herself.

'Why?' he questioned, pulling her back to him.

She laughed, shaking her head. 'You know all the reasons better than I do.'

'Business and pleasure don't mix?' he grinned as she took both his hands from her wrist.

She hurried back to her desk, a small frown on her forehead. 'Please?'

He lifted his shoulders in defeat. 'It's

going to be difficult leaving you alone. Still, I suppose I can manage to wait . . . '

She swallowed, her eyes trapped by his. He leaned across her desk, saying softly, 'There's only one thing I want to do. I want to make love to you, Mrs Shaw. You are the most delicious, sexy lady — '

'Luke!' She drew in a deep breath. 'Someone will hear!'

'Sorry,' he muttered, unrepentant. 'May I have some coffee? It smells almost as delicious as . . . ' He grinned, stopping before she could shout at him.

The effect of his tall body hidden under the white coat moving around the office, pouring coffee, was a temporary setback, the repercussions on her concentration disastrous for a full five minutes until he left.

Howard bade her good morning with a wry little smile, but perhaps, she reflected, that was her imagination, as was the terrible feeling that what she had done was comprehensively illustrated on her forehead — in luminous paint!

* * *

With Luke's disappearance at midday on a visit to a new mastitis outbreak, Sophie forced her mind back to the problem of Lucy.

Finishing the last of her office work, she drove out to the terraced cottage on the outskirts of Cranthorpe, hoping she would be able to resolve at least one of the staff problems today. If Lucy really was unfit then she would have to find a replacement.

Knocking on the red-painted door of the Freemans' home, she saw Lucy's freckled face appear. 'Come in! It's open!' she mouthed, raising a crutch to knock the latch open.

Sophie gasped in surprise at the cumbersome half-leg plaster.

'Oh, I'm getting used to it.' Lucy grinned, swivelling somehow to hobble in.

Sophie had known Lucy and her parents for years and they were devoted to horses, the field beyond the cottage home to two strawberry roans that the family had kept since Lucy was old enough to crawl.

'The specialist thinks I'll have it on for another three to four weeks,' Lucy sighed, levering the plaster up on a footstool. 'Fancy signing it?'

Sophie took the offered felt-tip and scrawled her name, glancing up to find Lucy studying her curiously. 'So, what's been happening while I've been away?'

'John's off with a viral infection. Did you know?'

Lucy shook her head. 'Haven't heard a thing. I was going to ask Luke last week when I saw him at the Cranthorpe Arms. I managed to hobble in for a drink with my boyfriend. Luke was there with a gorgeous-looking brunette, very chic, very sexy. I didn't feel like butting in. They seemed too preoccupied, if you know what I mean.'

Sophie felt as though she'd collided with a brick wall. Lucy glanced at her curiously, taking in her pale face. 'Oh, don't worry, it wasn't in office hours,' the girl assured her, misinterpreting her silence.

'So . . . we'll work on about a month?' Sophie managed to ask calmly, changing the subject. 'And if you're not mobile, perhaps you can help out in administration. The bookwork is piling up horrendously.'

'Great, can't wait!' Lucy pulled herself up. 'I'll die of boredom if I don't start getting out and about again.'

Sophie managed to walk to the door, saying her goodbyes without revealing, she hoped, how the remark about Luke and the brunette had affected her.

Pulling into a lay-by, she sat in silence. A little voice inside repeated, I told you so. What did you expect, Sophie Shaw? The charm that had melted her into bed had also worked in just the same way with other women.

Luke had made no promises, told her he had no intention of ever being anything other than a committed bachelor. But their lovemaking had made her feel so different — and not just their lovemaking, but afterwards; curling alongside his warm, strong body, his arms around her in sleep, had been blissful.

She had fallen headlong into the wild storm, emerged with a deep physical renewal she did not regret, but for Luke it had merely been a way to relax, his recipe, she thought bitterly, for a long and happy life.

A few short weeks she had known him and look what had happened. How could she expect him to think anything else but that she fully accepted his attitude towards sex, shortlived relationships . . . affairs?

If she didn't want to get hurt, she must stop before it was too late — unless, of course, she could regard it in the same way that he did. No strings, no commitments, no whispered words of love. After all, Luke did not know what love was — she had already worked that out for herself, well before she had allowed him to take her to bed.

Arriving at the house, she parked and

hurried in. As she picked up the phone she saw evidence of Luke all around . . . a wax jacket in the hall, boots at the door, after-shave pervading the house. Everything to remind her he had become a part of her life.

She made a quick call to Jane, telling her she was going to work in her small study at home.

Ten minutes later as she was about to leave the house the phone rang. It would be Luke, she knew. Swiftly she collected a sweater, ignored the ringing and slammed the door behind her.

★　★　★

'Where did you disappear to today?' Luke asked as she walked in that evening. He stood before her in pinny and sleeves rolled up. An acrid aroma floated from the kitchen.

He enfolded her into his arms. 'You weren't here when I came home. I missed you.'

She looked up into the deep blue

173

eyes, unable to resist their expression. 'I'll bet.'

He wrinkled his nose. 'Cynic.'

He sighed as he lifted her chin. 'What's up? Bad day?'

She shook her head. 'I've just been walking . . . thinking.'

He groaned. 'I told you thinking too much is bad for you.'

She moved, pressing her hands against him. 'I'm just not used to what I . . . to what we're doing. To coming home, finding you here — '

He gave a hollow laugh. 'You say the nicest things. How can you be so unkind to a man who slaves over the oven and manages to burn everything in sight?'

She smiled up into his mock-serious face. 'Is this a confession?'

He nodded. 'I cooked omelettes and ate mine because I was so ravenous and then I put yours in the oven and forgot about it. I plead guilty to the crime of egg incineration and have no excuse — other than the woman I wanted to see and touch and hold more than anyone else in the world had apparently deserted me.'

She laughed softly. 'You're hopeless.'

He kissed her mouth hungrily. 'Come and have a drink. I bought some wine and parsley for the eggs.' He propelled her into the kitchen. 'But as omelette is no longer on the menu, can I get you something else to cat?'

She giggled. 'You really did burn it?'

He nodded. 'To a crisp.' He drew her into his arms, pushing himself into the warm curve of her soft body. It responded immediately to the slow sensual movements of his hands over the small of her back. 'Let's take some wine to bed,' he whispered coaxingly, all but lifting her off her small feet.

She pressed her palms against his chest. 'Luke, today I decided . . . '

'I know what you decided,' he cut in, dropping his head to kiss her neck. 'This is the last time. Then I'll move back into my room and you can be respectable again.'

'I don't believe you,' she sighed, knowing it was really herself she couldn't convince, closing her eyes at the seductive pressure of his mouth.

At this moment she desired nothing more than to feel his strong body against her, melt beneath the sheets with him — despite the vow she had made this afternoon to keep him firmly out of her bed and, therefore, out of her heart.

She smiled up at him. 'You're impossible,' she whispered in despair.

'So you keep telling me.'

He swept her off her feet and up into his arms, pulling her roughly into his chest. 'And if you keep telling me I suppose I might just begin to believe it.'

He unbuttoned her blouse slowly and tugged it from the waistband of her skirt. With careful deliberation he laid her back on the bed and she undid his shirt as he bent over her, accepting the warm kisses he rained down on her face and neck.

Now there seemed a new dimension

176

to the acts that had happened before. Now she wanted to savour, to imprint each gesture in her mind; the feel of his body beneath the cotton shirt as she dragged it from his shoulders; the way his thighs hardened as their naked muscles gripped her body in a vice of need, her fingertips running smoothly over them, making them rise up under her touch.

He kissed her breasts, supporting them in his palms as she flicked open her eyes to see his lips move over them, as she arched, obedient to his demands, and heard him whisper gruffly, 'Oh, Sophie, I just can't help myself. You are so, so beautiful.'

Face taut with control, he lay back, closing his black-lashed eyelids to her enquiring fingertips, her lips lowering to the steady pulse in his neck, biting the skin beneath his dark beard and then to the smooth, sensitive area of his groin, discovering the instant response of his body to her provocative touch.

Quite when he lost control she

couldn't remember, as the words she wanted to say and did not trailed away on a broken sigh as at last he brought her to the ultimate with a cry of his own need, her body engulfed in a liquid heat as they rose together in rapturous unity.

★　★　★

They slept, she realised, for eight uninterrupted hours. At seven she was the first to rise, reluctantly leaving his warmth to shower and dress.

By the time she had brushed her hair and applied a light coat of lipstick he had risen to wrap his arms around her and wipe it off again, messing up her hair with playful hands, beginning to draw off the soft blouse that she had chosen for the day.

She stayed his fingers reluctantly. 'I have to go,' she murmured, fighting him gently away, aware that her hands were loath to relinquish the moist warmth of his body as he stood against her.

'You'll be there before me,' he

groaned, teasing amusement in his sleepy eyes. 'What apology are you going to make for me?'

'None,' she grinned, pushing back his hair, trailing her hands down his neck. 'Why should I?'

'It was your fault,' he complained, nodding to the ruffled bed. 'Some strange, exciting, savage woman accosted me in my sleep.'

She laughed. 'And you resisted her, of course!'

'With all my might.' He let her go on a sigh. 'You'd better be on your way, I suppose.'

She must, she told herself as she walked into the fresh, clear day, try to keep everything in perspective. This was just a fling in Luke's eyes; as cruel as it might seem, it was the truth. Memorable at best for him, merely added to the scrapbook at worst.

Out of her depth? Yes. But she had already become addicted. Her decision to stop before anything got started had been abandoned the moment she had walked back in last night.

She was too weak to fight it.

Desire stabbed through her as she thought of their lovemaking. Not lovemaking in the literal sense of the word to Luke, perhaps, but to her, yes.

God help her, flouting all common sense, all logic, she couldn't help herself. She was falling in love.

7

Under an avalanche of early-morning casualties, Sophie found herself cornering a spitting marmalade tom cat, who, having escaped the reception area, secreted himself in the cupboard used for cleaning equipment.

'He's just been in a fight,' his owner, a lady in a headscarf, cried as she fought to reach him between the mops and brooms.

'Poor thing,' Sophie murmured sympathetically. 'He's probably terrified.'

'You're joking! You ought to see the other cat . . . torn to ribbons.'

With a graphic account of the cat fight going on in her left ear, Sophie took out a pair of durable cleaning gloves. 'In that case, I think you'd better have these.'

'What's all the noise?' Howard asked as the tom and owner battled it out.

Sophie grinned. 'A rather unwilling patient. Will you see him next, Howard?'

The tom was finally captured as the woman threw a large yellow duster over his head and grabbed him. Howard frowned at Sophie as they came into his consulting-room. 'No Luke?'

She looked up. 'Yes, he — er — was delayed just a few minutes. He'll be here shortly.'

'This cat's a monster,' the woman interrupted them, depositing the gaggle of furry legs on the examination bench. 'He's so antisocial that my neighbours call him Frankie Frankenstein.'

Howard raised an eyebrow. 'Are you going to be able to control him, or am I going to have to give him something to calm him down? What's going to make life easiest?'

'As soon as I take this duster off he'll go crazy,' the client answered without hesitation.

'Right,' Howard sighed. 'A small jab, then; hold him still.'

The swift injection of tranquilliser

given, Frankie soon calmed, the spitting and hissing subsiding to a soft mewing and finally silence.

The woman gingerly unfolded the duster. Frankie's green eyes still glimmered, but he made no attempt to escape.

'You can do without the gloves, I think,' Howard told the woman as he carefully ran his hands over Frankie's soft fur.

After a careful examination, Howard pointed to the bloodstained tear along the ridge of his spine. 'This will need four or five stitches . . . not too bad really. There's a cut on his nose and over his eye, but they will heal.'

Sophie cleaned the wound and Howard administered a local anaesthetic. 'Have you thought of having him neutered?' he asked the woman. 'It could help his behavioural problem; stop all this kind of thing.'

'But will he still catch rats?' she demanded suspiciously.

Howard shrugged. 'No reason why he

shouldn't. Might even make him a better ratter, since he won't feel like leaving his territory to seek out fights.'

Somewhat mollified, she brooked no further argument and Sophie sprinkled antibiotic powder from a spatula, preparing the suturing needle while they waited for the anaesthetic to take.

A half-dozen neat stitches later, Howard patted a tripping Frankie. 'Just an intramuscular injection and it's all over. Now, what's it to be?' he asked firmly. 'Do you want Frankie re-upholstered? If so, we'll keep him in and attend to him in the morning.'

'I'm bringing him back if he stops his ratting,' the client threatened, wagging a finger.

Howard merely grinned, rubbing an index finger softly behind Frankie's ear as she departed. 'Not that we'll be able to do much about the ratting after he's done,' he chuckled, thrusting a hand through his grey hair, 'but it will give the neighbours a break if nothing else.' He took the cat in his arms and went to deliver him safely to a recovery cage.

'How does it go at home?' he asked her on his return, watching her with interest as she sponged down the bench for the next patient.

She nodded. 'Fine, thanks, Howard.'

'No problems?'

She looked up, sighing as she straightened her back. Howard knew her so well that she couldn't lie, but at the same time she couldn't bring herself to discuss Luke.

The older vet shrugged. 'We were wondering how you were managing, that's all, my dear. Molly keeps asking me,' he added with a wry smile.

Sophie smiled. 'Tell Molly not to worry. I'm coping. It's a long time since I've had company in the house — but yes, it's OK.'

Howard stared at her for a long while. 'You know you can talk to me, Sophie, if ever there's a problem? I feel rather responsible for Luke. After all, it was me who was so keen to take him on. After Michael — ' Howard stopped as a tap came at the door and Imelda appeared.

'Sorry to interrupt,' she apologised flusteredly, 'but I'm looking for Luke.'

Sophie frowned. 'He'll be in at any moment. Can I help, Imelda?'

The young nurse hesitated. 'There's a lady on the phone, says it's personal — insists on speaking to Luke. Sounds a bit upset.'

'Someone asking for me?' a deep voice called, and Imelda spun around.

'Oh, Luke, I've a call for you . . . '

'Switch it through to my room. I'll take it in there,' Sophie heard and was surprised when he avoided greeting them as he normally would and disappeared to his phone call.

'Trouble?' Howard asked as Sophie jerked her head back to stare at him.

'I wouldn't know,' she sighed.

Howard grinned. 'Women usually do.' He slid an arm around her shoulders. 'If it's any consolation, despite Luke's domestic upheavals, he really is proving himself a rather spectacular partner. He's taken

186

over most of John's clients, doesn't turn a hair — he's popular with the farms too. I can't fault him.'

She nodded. 'Yes, he's quite brilliant.'

Finally leaving Howard to his next patient, she went slowly back to the office, noting that Luke's door was firmly closed.

Whether she liked it or not, she would have to content herself with the situation. Was it Amanda Drew or Patricia De Vere? she couldn't help wondering. Lucy had seen him at the Cranthorpe Arms with a brunette. Yet he never talked of any of the women in his life, nor had she asked.

Pride held her back, she supposed. Pride and fear that she might discover yet another reason why she should not be embarking on an affair which could only bring her certain heartache.

*   *   *

Over a week later Sophie finally accepted Hamish Burns's invitation to dinner.

Pressed beyond her resolution to avoid the duty, she finally weakened, wishing as he walked from her office that she had had the courage to refuse the mandatory offer.

Returning to the house at six, Sophie set out a salad, quiche and cold potatoes for Luke. He arrived home, his cords and boots covered in farmyard filth. Obligingly he left his boots on the doorstep and was stripping off his jerkin as he entered the hall.

'You're looking very lovely this evening,' he murmured as he stood before her, his broad shoulders flexed as he stretched, depositing the muddied sweater in a discreet heap behind the door.

His declaration to make her respectable had held only because he was on call in John's absence, she had realised. After the phone call she had seized the opportunity to distance herself as if she was afraid to let him get too close, retiring early to bed, struggling with her own conflicting emotions, listening for the sound of his footfall as he passed her door, wondering just what she would do if he called to her.

Now she had come downstairs, realising this was the first time they had arrived in the house together for days. She wanted to reach up and rub the tired lines from the corners of his eyes, smooth her thumb pads over his temples and wipe away the exhaustion of the last few days.

His eyes ran over the midnight-blue silk dress, moulding her slender body under its softly cut silk. His voice was low as he came slowly towards her. 'Oh, Sophie, you look beautiful.'

He took her into his arms, dragging her from the last stair, her last line of resistance gone as she felt the warmth and strength of his body. 'You know, this is ridiculous,' he whispered tiredly, his mouth sinking into her hair. 'Don't shut me out. Don't pretend what happened between us didn't happen. Sophie, I miss you, I want to hold you — '

'Luke, you don't understand,' she murmured weakly into his shoulder. 'I can't handle things so easily. You make it all sound so simple . . . '

He held her tighter. 'But it is, isn't it?'

Her breath stopped in her chest. How could she tell him if he didn't know? She was in love, so deeply in love. Nothing made sense any more, not the nights with him, nor those without him.

'I want you,' he murmured, stroking her hair. 'I want you so much. That seems pretty straightforward to me.'

She sighed, trying to mask the pain in her voice. 'It would to you.'

He prised her from him, looking deeply into her eyes. Slowly a grin came over his lips. 'Tonight I've no surgery and I'm not on call . . . '

She bit her lip. 'Luke, I'm going out.'

She saw the sudden surprise in his face, though he tried to hide it. 'Oh?' he said, letting her go. 'I should have guessed.' His eyes went over the dress.

'You wouldn't have worn this for staying at home, would you?' He paused, searching her face. 'Who with? Anyone I know?'

'Just a meal on behalf of the pharmaceutical company. I've been putting it off for so long — '

'Hamish?' he said flatly.

She nodded, aware of the coolness of his tone. 'I won't be late.'

He smiled tiredly, letting go of her. 'I'm all in anyway. I thought I'd get an early night.'

'Luke?' She reached out as he went to walk away. 'I'm sorry.'

He looked back at her with a shrug. 'This is the first night I've had free. I would like to have spent it with you.'

Sophie's brown eyes widened. 'Would you?'

He frowned. 'Of course I would.' He spun back, taking her arms in a hard grasp between his fingers, suddenly angry. 'Sophie, what the hell do you want from me? You know how I feel about you.'

She shook her head. 'I don't know, Luke. That's just it. I'm not sure what we have between us — if there's anything at all.'

He shook his head, narrowing his eyes. 'I can't give you any guarantees of undying love, if that's what you mean. I'm not Michael,' he told her roughly. 'I told you, Sophie, I'm a bachelor, I'm made that way. It would be unkind of me to pretend anything else . . . what we've shared between us isn't wrong unless you felt it was wrong.'

'You mean sex?' she asked, staring at him numbly. 'What we have is sex?'

He made a small growling noise as her heart seemed to drop. 'Don't demean us, Sophie.'

'I . . . I can only explain what I feel.' She gazed at him bleakly. 'It's as though I don't know where I am, as though I'm lost . . . I don't know how to handle — us.' A tear crept from the corner of her eye and suddenly his angry face softened as he wiped it gently away.

'Oh, hell,' he muttered and pulled her

gently to him, sending a spasm of need through her as she closed her eyes and buried her head in his shoulder. 'I don't want to hurt you, Sophie. We're both tired,' he whispered as he held her. After a while he pushed her gently away, raising an eyebrow. 'Hadn't you better be getting ready for your date?'

She sighed, forcing back the tears. 'It's not a date. You know that.'

'But does Hamish Burns?' he remarked drily, letting her go. 'And, the way you're looking tonight, I don't see how the man can keep his hands off you.'

She took a deep breath, blushing despite herself. She wondered what he would say if she confronted him about the women he was seeing, the women who seemed to slip in and out of his life like shadows and whom he seemed to be quite content never to discuss.

Sophie couldn't bring herself to do it. But one question she had been too frightened to ask herself appeared resolved no matter how much it hurt to accept: Luke was a confirmed bachelor and that was the way he intended to stay.

★ ★ ★

Hamish Burns rang the bell, the shadow of his tall blond form hovering outside the frosted glass of the front door.

Luke stepped aside as she pushed back the hair from her face, her large brown eyes reflecting the discreet dazzle of the tiny pearls in her ears.

Luke gazed at her as they faced each other in the hall, his eyes pinned to her with a stomach-tumbling expression of intense blue.

'Your date,' he muttered, one black eyebrow quirking up. 'Don't keep the man waiting.'

'Luke — ' She swallowed, the words dying in her throat. Her heart hammered as she forced herself to move and open the door. Hamish wore an elegant dark suit and smiled, only to lose the warmth from his expression as his gaze went to Luke by the stairs.

Sophie felt her cheeks swim with colour as the two men stared at one another. 'Hello, Hamish,' she mumbled, aware that the temperature had dropped disastrously. Collecting her purse from the table and hurrying past Luke, she gave him a strained smile.

'Enjoy yourselves,' he drawled smoothly.

Sophie hurried to the red Saab, Hamish opening the door for her to slide in, relieved when he finally started the engine and drove away.

'I'm sorry,' he murmured quietly after a while. 'I had no idea you had company.'

'Luke is staying at the house while he finds a property.' Feeling she should clarify the situation to avoid more questioning by Hamish, she added coolly, 'The bungalow was damaged in the storm and needs extensive repairs.'

'Lucky fellow,' Hamish replied drily and Sophie felt a sudden pang of annoyance at the innuendo.

Managing to steer the conversation

away from personal issues, she was relieved when they finally arrived at the restaurant.

The country hotel offered a wide selection of good, traditional food and Sophie chose the roast beef while Hamish opted for steak. The talk between them constituted more of a business meeting than a social occasion and she was pleased to keep it that way. She had no intention of bringing up the subject of Luke again and was surprised when, after coffee, Hamish circled the rim of his cup pensively.

'Don't you ever get bored with just the practice day after day, Sophie?' he asked curiously.

She shrugged. 'Michael and I put everything we had into the practice — it's a way of life.'

'I know you and Michael never had much time for socialising,' he agreed thoughtfully. 'I thought — ' He stopped, looking under his lashes at her. 'Well, I can see what the attraction is at home now. I hadn't realised.'

Sophie snapped up her eyes. 'I'm sorry?'

He lifted his shoulders. 'Look, I know it's none of my business, but there has been talk circulating about your new partner — '

'Gossip, you mean?' Sophie cut in angrily.

'Not that it's necessarily true,' he told her calmly. 'I'm just concerned — for your sake. I don't want to see you hurt,' he persisted, stretching his hand across the table. Squeezing her fingers, he said softly, 'I'm very fond of you, Sophie.'

She saw the message clearly written in his eyes. For the first time since she had ever known him, Sophie was uncomfortable in his presence. 'Hamish, I like you too.' She drew away her hand, leaving him staring after it. 'And I value your friendship . . . '

'But?'

'I hope we'll always be friends.'

He laughed hollowly. 'Just friends?'

She wondered why she could not have

responded to someone like Hamish, good-looking and fun to be with, but the touch of his hand had left her wishing she had not agreed to go out with him this evening, Luke's observation proving to be embarrassingly accurate.

'I really feel quite shattered, Hamish,' she began hesitantly. 'You know how pressed we've been at the practice this week with the mastitis outbreak.'

'You're saying it's time I took you home?' His soft blond eyebrows rose. 'What a pity.'

Sophie realised he was trying to disguise the effect of her clumsy rebuff. 'I really am sorry,' she added quietly, aware by his expression that she was only making things worse.

The tension of the homeward journey was alleviated only by Sophie's concerted effort to keep the conversation going, Hamish unwilling to lend much effort to the task.

As he pulled the Saab to a halt outside the house Sophie breathed a silent sigh of relief. 'Thank you for a lovely evening,' she said, trying to sound as though she really had enjoyed it.

'Can I invite myself in for a nightcap?' The unexpected request came as he glanced at the house and the lights burning on the bottom floor. Suddenly he turned to face her, slipping an arm along the back of her seat, stretching his other hand out to grasp hers. 'We really haven't had much time to get to know one another in a personal sense, Sophie. We might find we have a lot more in common than we think.' He pulled her to him, his breath hot on her face.

Too late she tried to push him away, his mouth coming down to cover hers. 'Hamish, don't!' she cried, forcing her hands against his chest.

He looked at her first in surprise, then, as she managed to find the handle and pull herself away, anger spread across his face. 'I suppose your guest of honour demands your undivided attention?' he threw at her sarcastically as she clambered out on shaky legs.

'That's entirely my business, Hamish,' she called back before she slammed the door.

She hurried from the car, her lips stinging from the rough kiss, her heart beating rapidly. She hadn't bargained for Hamish's behaviour — he certainly hadn't ever given her the impression he would not treat her with respect. But then, she had always avoided accepting the invitation from his company, and had she not been so preoccupied with her feelings for Luke perhaps she would have realised that there had always been an element of risk in going out with Hamish alone.

The door opened in front of her as she went to slot in her key. Luke frowned at her expression. 'Are you all right?' he asked in a low voice.

She nodded, unaware that the Saab had not yet moved off. Luke's face clouded as he looked towards the car.

'Are you sure?' he asked her with growing concern.

She nodded. 'Yes, really, I'm fine. Let's get in.'

Luke lingering longer than was necessary before he closed the door, Sophie heard the engine start up and the angry roar of a car accelerating at unnecessary speed.

Luke closed the door. 'Your friend is in a hurry,' he murmured tightly.

Sophie sighed, dropping her purse to the hall table. 'Yes, I suppose he is.'

Suddenly she was in his arms and his hands were in her hair, his lips coming down over hers with hungry need. 'Missed you,' he whispered huskily, kissing her again and again until she had to put her hands up and hold his face still. His skin was warm and soft under her touch, the dark growth of beard springing up from its surface with masculine strength, prickling against her fingertips.

'And I missed you,' she whispered back, tempted to laugh, the feeling of

201

lightheadedness sweeping over her.

'I've made coffee,' he grunted, chewing at her ear.

She giggled. 'You knew what time I'd be home?'

He grinned, kissing her nose. 'I was coming out to look for you if you weren't in by eleven.'

'You sound like my father.'

'I don't feel like it.'

'Kiss me again,' she whispered, so relieved to be in his arms that her heart thumped wildly in happiness.

No further words were needed between them as his mouth marauded her body and he slipped the dainty straps from her pale shoulders, sinking his teeth into her skin to lick and nibble her soft flesh.

'Take me to bed,' she managed to whisper, her hands pulling open his cotton shirt, dragging carelessly on the buttons, her nails driving into the thick black hair that sprang from his tightly muscled chest.

'You're sure?' he breathed, holding

her head between his hands. 'You're not going to have all those doubts again in the morning?'

'I probably will.' There was no 'probably' about it, she knew she would, but now she didn't care any more.

'My God, Sophie . . . what are we going to do?' For a moment he stiffened, frowning deeply as she felt his heart beat against his chest.

'Make love,' she said softly, her brown eyes heavy with need. 'And cross the bridge of tomorrow when it comes.'

He smiled lazily. 'Mrs Metaphor. How can I resist you?' He slid the dress from her body and it fell around her ankles. He stretched out a long arm and thrust his palm against the light switch. In darkness he ran his hands over her body, bending his head to kiss the creamy soft slope of her breasts. 'Beautiful,' he whispered, nuzzling into them, caressing them with his tongue, smoothing and sucking their pouting buds as she arched with desire and he lifted her from her feet, her long legs twisting around his waist.

*   *   *

'Breakfast,' Luke grinned, setting the tray down beside the bed. Sophie woke to the sight of the lean, muscular body swathed in a pocket-sized handtowel tugged around his waist standing above her, and the smell of freshly brewed coffee in the air.

'What time is it?' She almost swung her legs out of bed until she realised it would have been indecent. Covering herself with the sheet, she saw Luke laughing at her.

'Don't panic!' He sat down beside her and, kissing her, took her flushed face in his hands. 'It's only seven-thirty. Besides, it's Saturday. I'm in this morning, but you don't have to come along — Jane's there. Why don't you stay in bed? Then perhaps when I come home at lunchtime we can continue where we left off last night?'

204

'Idiot,' she grinned, relaxing as she realised it was the weekend. 'It wasn't last night,' she reminded him teasingly, 'it was early this morning.' She munched at the toast he pushed between her teeth. 'May I have some marmalade?' she pouted, licking the crumbs from her lips.

'Couldn't find it,' he grumbled. 'Stop complaining and eat up.'

Mouth full, she obeyed, remembering as she ate the bliss of their lovemaking, the way he had caressed every inch of her body down to the last and least of exciting extremities, which she now wiggled under the sheet.

He grinned wickedly. 'You look very moreish. I wonder, is there time for dessert?'

'You've just had breakfast; I can tell by the crumbs around your mouth,' she giggled, curling her feet. 'You're a glutton, do you know that?'

'You can talk!'

She blushed deeply, remembering vividly her uninhibited responses, hiding her embarrassment now by sipping her coffee and lowering her eyes. She had never realised how much she could respond when it came to loving someone physically, recalling with shame her hungry desire, drawing the last of his strength as she had ventured over the long, enticing body that now lazed beside her.

What had he thought? she wondered, her colour deepening. She had delighted him over and over again throughout the night, until the grey light of dawn had broken in through the window and they had drifted off to sleep, her melted body curled in the warm circle of his arms.

'Don't you think you should put something on?' she giggled, flicking up her blonde lashes.

He grinned as he stroked her partially covered breast under the sheet. 'Temptress,' he growled.

She blushed, placing the cup back on its saucer, afraid to meet his amused gaze. 'You'll be late — '

'Who cares?

She laughed softly. 'Your clients.'

He sighed, running his eyes over the soft curve of her body under the sheet. 'Enjoy your breakfast. Keep my space warm.'

She watched him go, her eyes lingering on the neat, smooth outline of his buttocks beneath the towel arranged scantily around his slim hips. His broad shoulders swayed above, in rhythm with the long, slow strides he took across the floor.

Sophie showered and dressed slowly, savouring the new sense of abandonment she felt, realising that, in losing her battle with Luke, she had won another. Luke had been right when he had said the ghosts of the past had needed to be exorcised. Last night she had finally done that, knowing the past was over and that all her present and, she hoped, some of her future lay beside her.

Her marriage had been carved from Michael's roots, not hers. Her want for a child had been swallowed up in the practice and she had begun to realise that Michael would never have willingly given in to her having a baby.

She might have achieved motherhood by more devious means, but Michael would never have forgiven her. It would have seemed like a betrayal for him.

The realisation of this was what caused her to argue with him, like peeling away layers of a wound that would never heal. There had been no compromise in Michael's angry eyes on the night he had died. She had known that when he returned from the visit the gulf between them would widen yet again, the panacea to their personal differences the practice.

Blinking in the mirror, Sophie abandoned the unhappy thoughts and gazed across from the bedroom window to the gleaming conicals. Luke had inspired hope in her. Could she inspire it in him? Could she convince him there was a future for them together?

Her heart quailing at the prospect, she suddenly needed to be in his company to feel the reassurance of his presence. The house was too lonely . . .

Impetuously deciding to go into work, she dressed in a soft silk blouse of palest blue, sliding on smooth cotton denims and summer sandals. Ten minutes later she was walking towards the practice, wondering what excuse she was going to give Jane for turning up on a Saturday morning and not really caring that she didn't have one. Her lighthearted frame of mind lasted until she pushed open the surgery door.

The small woman looked up as Sophie entered, her face puffy and swollen. The man standing next to her Sophie recognised, his tall frame hovering over his wife as she bade them good morning.

'Not good as far as we're concerned,' Mr Farley grunted.

'What's happened? Is it Siegfried?' she asked anxiously, her heart beginning to sink.

'You'd best ask that new vet of yours

what the trouble is!' the man exclaimed angrily.

Leaving the Farleys, she hurried along to Luke's consulting-room. Jane caught her arm as she raised her hand to knock on the door.

'Sophie, I think you should know what happened before you see Luke.'

Sophie nodded. 'A disagreement on Siegfriend's treatment?'

Jane hesitated, keeping her voice low. 'Luke helped the Farleys carry Siegfried in from their car. Mr Farley shouted at him, telling him he blamed the dog's illness on the medication, that it was mismanagement of his condition. He also said that he was going to complain to the authorities if Siegfried died.'

Sophie sighed. 'All right, Jane, thank you. I'll go and see what's happened.' In her heart she sensed what the outcome would be and, tapping lightly on the door, she went in.

Luke turned to look at her, folding up his stethoscope and digging it deep into his pocket.

'A massive second heart attack. He was dead on arrival.'

Sophie nodded, going to stand by him, her eyes going down to the lifeless form on the examination table. 'It was a battle you couldn't win, Luke,' she told him quietly. 'He would have had a year, maybe eighteen months at the most. You did everything you could and more.'

She felt her heart ache for him. Final defeat was never easy to come to terms with and she knew that in Siegfried's case, unless the treatment had been started much earlier, the chances of survival at his age, with progressive heart disease, were very small. It was always a trauma losing a patient, even more so if the owner's grief was as volatile and misplaced as Mr Farley's.

'Well, I'd better see them,' he said tightly. 'Though I think they'll find it hard to accept.'

An observation she could entirely agree with when the man burst into angry abuse as Luke delivered the news.

'You are entitled to complain to the Veterinary Council if you wish,' Luke agreed calmly, the bitter insult of their threat to report his treatment of their dog tightening his profile as he refused to return the man's anger.

'If you'd left well enough alone he'd still be here today.' Mr Farley turned and, leaving his wife, thrust open the door. Sophie's heart softened as she saw the woman's tear-streaked face.

'Once you have both recovered from your shock,' she said reasonably, 'I'm sure your husband will see reason. Mr Jordon kept Siegfried under night-and-day observation before he was discharged. Nothing more could have been done, by us or any other veterinary surgeon.'

Mrs Farley dried her eyes with a tissue and, surprisingly, thanked them. When she had gone Sophie glanced at Luke to discover his face grey and hollowed.

'Thank you for the vote of confidence,' he murmured in husky tones. 'Did you mean it? Or was it just practice policy, defending the workforce?'

Sophie shook her head, shocked. 'It was the truth, of course.'

With Jane present she could not reach out and draw him into her arms as she dearly wanted to, realising, though he tried not to show it, that his professional pride had been deeply wounded.

8

The call came through as they arrived back at the house.

Sophie picked up the phone and listened to a voice she had never heard before, understanding after a while that this was Louise, Luke's sister.

'For you,' she called and Luke took the phone, catching hold of her hand, tugging her towards him as he talked. She could feel the vibration of his voice as she leaned against his chest, smell the warmth permeate his body as she pressed her face down into the white shirt.

'I'll come as soon as I can,' she heard him say. He replaced the phone and slowly turned her in his arms. 'Pip, my niece, has been taken into hospital. She was knocked down by a car last night as she went to her Guides meeting.'

'Oh, Luke! Is she — ?'

'She's a tough little thing.' His face was strained now. 'I'm sure she'll be OK, but I have to go. Louise and Martin will need all the support they can get.'

Sophie nodded. 'Is there anything I can do?'

He took her head between his hands. 'Will you be able to cope, is more to the point. We'll need a locum.'

'Maybe John's feeling better.'

'I'll ring him.' He lifted his shoulders in a gesture of helplessness. 'I have to go.'

'Of course you do.' She asked softly, 'When?'

'Tomorrow. In the morning they are transferring her to Cambridge General from their local one.'

She slipped her hands into his and kissed them, looking at him under her long lashes. 'I'm so sorry about Siegfried. You know, what that man said was said in anger. He was just taking his grief out on the nearest person and it happened to be you.'

He shrugged. 'Who knows? It still doesn't make you feel any the less responsible.'

She nodded, slipping her hands behind his neck. 'And now this.' She looked into his worried face and smiled. 'Feeling hungry, by any chance?'

His lips twisted in the semblance of a grin. 'For you, yes. But if that's not on offer, I'll eat a sandwich.'

She laughed, more from relief that he was managing to joke. 'Go and sit down — I'll bring something in on a tray for us.'

He turned to the drawing-room, then hesitated, running a hand through his hair tiredly. 'I'll think I'll ring John first, get the surgery sorted out.'

An hour later she sat beside him on the sofa, her head resting in the crook of his arm, his fingers gently caressing her hair. It was a tender stroke, a gentle, loving gesture, and she reached up to kiss him on the mouth. 'I'll miss you,' she whispered, meaning it more than he could ever know.

He drew her fully into the cradle of his lap, leaning her head on the sofa arm, stroking the silky stands of blonde hair from her forehead. 'What do you want to do now?' he asked ruefully. 'Or need I ask?'

She blushed. Had the day continued as it had begun, they would be at this moment safely in one another's arms in bed, having considered no other alternative. But Siegfried's death and Pip's accident and its implications had left them both feeling in a strange mood.

'How about a walk, get some fresh air?' she asked uncertainly.

'Good idea.' His face relaxed and she knew she had made the right suggestion. Luke's was a strong face, she thought as she studied him from where she lay, square jawed with a dark, sexy stubble just beginning to form. His night-black hair had fallen forward and a little pulse worked in the base of his jaw. 'Come on. Before we change our minds,' he coaxed.

Sandwiches left half eaten, taking

Steamer in the Jaguar with them, they drove into the country and walked for hours along the winding lanes that skirted Cranthorpe.

They knew their stroll was no more than an exercise to distract them from what had happened and the inevitability of his departure. But then as they walked, he began to tell her more of his childhood and of the days after his parents' divorce.

His father, a top barrister working in the City, had seemed a distant figure, and his mother, involved deeply with her charity work, was a woman more preoccupied with her own life than her children's. The relationship he had enjoyed with his father after the divorce had been civil but sporadic and, at times, cool, while his mother had remarried again and saw less and less of her two children.

Gregory Jordon's disapproval of his son's choice of profession had set up yet another hurdle in their lukewarm relationship and had grown over the years into polite indifference. His father had never remarried and had died before Luke had returned from his travels abroad.

With each small revelation Sophie began to understand more the bewildered boy and then the rebellious adolescent Luke had grown into.

How had he coped with the alienation from love and affection? She supposed he projected the same defences into adulthood as he had done when he was a child. Tough they might be and had held in place for thirty-three years, but, in the last few weeks, dared she hope that they had been slowly coming down as they had begun to know one another better?

He made love to her that evening with a desperation that frightened her. It was ridiculous to feel this way, she told herself as she watched him in his sleep, long lashes lying peacefully on high cheekbones. He would come home.

Home, Sophie thought as she lay next to him, seeking assurance from his sleeping face.

Home was where the heart was.

Was he near to loving her? She didn't know. Their affair, though she hated to think of it as that, was based on his terms. Enjoy life while you had it, he had told her, and had made no pretence of feeling otherwise, nor promised her more.

★　★　★

In Luke's absence John returned to work; though feeling jaded, he managed his surgeries well enough, and with a rare turn of luck, Sophie decided, the mastitis outbreak seemed to have been contained. With no more cases reported and Lucy calling to say she would return in a couple of weeks, the work front was looking up.

Domestically, though, it was another matter. The house felt bleak and lonely, with Luke's possessions still scattered around a sharp reminder of his absence. He was part of the house and everything in it echoed him. Even Steamer waited by the back door for his walks, which Luke had undertaken most mornings.

She missed him.

She missed the way he teased her and made her laugh, she missed him in her bed and in her arms, ached for his lovemaking, his tenderness and passion and the warmth of waking to find him lying alongside her.

He rang early in the week to say Pip had shown small but hopeful signs of recovery. The second time he rang Pip's condition was improved.

With such wonderful news Sophie tried to tell him how much she missed him, but it was difficult over the phone, as if the distancing of miles had distanced them emotionally. He had in some way closed himself off, she felt.

She accepted it must be the strain he

was under, for she knew he cared for Louise and Martin and Pip — passionately. But in her heart of hearts she worried how it would be for them when he returned.

To compound her unease, during the week Amanda Drew walked into Reception and asked for Luke. Jane called Sophie and she explained briefly that Luke had taken time off. The girl was beautiful, she thought again. She could be little more than twenty and yet her attitude was so confident and self-assured. Sophie watched her leave, a dragging sensation at the pit of her stomach as she wondered about the relationship between her and Luke.

Then on the Friday, the day before Luke was due to phone again, Patricia De Vere and her dog, Maroc, arrived at the surgery.

Sophie was discussing the rota for the following week should Luke not return, when her eyes flew up to meet Patricia's.

The actress, resplendent in a dramatic black suit, swept towards them. Sophie managed to avoid the amusement in Jane's eyes as heads in the surgery turned simultaneously.

The news that Patricia kept horses, one in particular that needed Luke's undivided and immediate attention, somehow did not surprise Sophie.

'Don't you have a regular vet?' she asked hesitantly.

Giving her a look of disdain, Patricia tossed back her long dark hair. 'Luke's marvellous with India. I wouldn't dream of anyone else touching her.'

Sophie said she would pass on the message, explaining that she wasn't sure when Luke would be back. She had the same heart-sinking sensation that always made her aware she knew next to nothing of Luke's life, an impression which Patricia De Vere did nothing to dispel as she insisted Sophie visit Longhaven, 'To be shown the house.'

Fortunately a rush of ailing small

animals distracted Sophie from further conversation.

'Looks like you've a free ticket for a grand tour,' Jane giggled as Patricia left.

'I think I'll pass on that one,' Sophie sighed and made a mental note to avoid the place like the plague.

When all the surgery casualties were dealt with Sophie slipped on a protective lead apron to help John in X-Ray. She was glad the day had been busy or she would have spent the best part thinking about Luke and the women in his life, reflecting with painful honesty that she now appeared to be one of them!

The dog was a Labrador with suspected hip dysplasia, and after giving a general anaesthetic Sophie helped to clamp the animal in a cradle on its back, supported by a moving grid. As she carefully took the radiographs it became clear through the development of the film that the dog could be treated with NSAIDs — non-steroidal anti-inflammatory drugs.

John glanced up at Sophie as they released the Labrador from his position and turned him gently on his side. 'No news from Luke, I suppose?' he asked casually.

Sophie shrugged. 'Pip hasn't sustained internal injuries as far as they can gather, but they're doing more tests.'

'Limbs broken?' John asked matter of factly.

'Her left arm, some scratching and bruising . . . she's been lucky so far. The motorist was slowing down, not increasing speed as he hit her.'

'With luck, then, he'll be home soon.'

Sophie cast him a fleeting look as they removed the dog to a recovery cage. It was a strange remark to make. Had he guessed they were having an affair? But she could tell nothing from his expression, their conversation returning to work and more mundane matters.

She wondered again that evening, as she made herself a snack, if John knew.

If any of the staff knew. Howard, she thought, had sensed her feelings long ago. She had known him too long for him not to read her like a book.

For once in her life she had sent caution to the wind. She realised she didn't care what people thought. She only knew she missed Luke so much that she wanted him back on any terms.

A decision that was instantly reaffirmed the moment he walked in the door on Saturday afternoon.

Sophie had been waiting for his call, but to see him standing there in the flesh sent all her sensations into chaos and she rushed into his arms, breathing in his familiar aroma, erupting inside with silent joy as he kissed her hungrily.

No words said, just a mumbled apology for not letting her know he was coming and that Pip was on the road to recovery, she found herself appalled at her immediate submission as he took her to bed.

★ ★ ★

Hours later she stood in a warm towelling robe, frying eggs.

Luke threaded his arms around her waist as she cooked, his unshaven beard nuzzling her cheek. 'I can remember doing this once before,' he murmured as he nibbled her ear, causing her to drop the egg from the spatula, tutting as it pancaked across the base of the frying-pan.

'Only it wasn't an egg I dropped, it was a very expensive bottle of plonk,' she laughed, squirming.

He nibbled the other ear, removing his hands from her waist to her back and kneading her shoulder-blades, making her groan with pleasure. 'That's wonderful,' she breathed, closing her eyes at the sensation of his fingers attacking her knotted shoulder muscles.

She gave up with the eggs and, flicking off the gas, turned to thread her arms around his neck.

'You're delicious,' he groaned, kissing her mouth. 'Can I eat you up? I've been trying hard enough for the past four hours but you won't stay still.'

Sophie blushed at the memory of their passionate lovemaking and the intimacies she had allowed him to take with full co-operation on her part.

'You keep wriggling away,' he complained, his hands slipping down to wrap her into him. 'A tasty little morsel you are, m'dear . . . ' he mimicked, his hands slinking to the V of her robe, there to be caught up by her own small fingers as they covered the full swell of her breast.

'You're stopping my fun — that's not in the rules,' he objected sullenly.

'You never keep to the rules. This is the kitchen. We're supposed to be eating,' she reminded him testily.

'I never cheat! Well, maybe one exception, like this lovely, sexy lady who I just can't leave alone — ' He grabbed her again and her body responded as they laughed, the pleasure of his hands running over her too sweet to dissuade, too much of a relief that everything between them for the moment was all right.

Breathlessly trapped in a corner, she wrapped her hands around his neck and gazed into his blue eyes, feeling the heat of his body as he leaned on her.

'Oh, darling,' she breathed huskily, longing to say the words she knew she mustn't. Swallowing, she looked up at him, her feelings written in her eyes. Was it her imagination that the pressure of his body against her lessened, stiffened even, as the silence grew?

'Let's eat those eggs before they turn back into chickens,' he suggested, his lips fleetingly brushing her cheek.

Why had she almost let it slip how she felt? she asked herself angrily as they broke apart to sit at the table. To tell him she loved him would be wrong, would ruin everything. Yet she needed to say it. She had hoped during their eager reunion that he would have whispered it, but he hadn't and now the atmosphere had cooled.

They ate scrambled eggs and toast, and peaches drowned in cream, the only supplies she had left in the house, having intended to shop today. Not at all sorry that she had swopped her trip to the supermarket for the delicious hours in bed, she watched him devour everything in sight before she next spoke.

'Amanda and Patricia have both been in to see you this week,' she murmured as she sipped her coffee.

He looked up, licking his lips. 'Interesting.'

'Patricia wants you to see one of her horses. She says you know the case well.'

'The plot thickens.'

'Luke, be serious.'

'I am.' He laughed as he reached across to catch her hand. 'Not jealous, by any chance?'

'Of course not. As a matter of fact she invited me out to Longhaven too.' Sophie could have bitten out her tongue. She had no desire to see the place and least of all to sound as if she did.

It was too late. Luke raised a speculative eyebrow. 'Did she, now? Then you must come.'

Sophie avoided answering. 'Tell me about your sister and her family,' she evaded, not daring to meet the amused blue eyes.

Sophie was well aware of the affection Luke had for his sister and her daughter and he began slowly to unfold the details of Pip's recovery, her waking from unconsciousness and the moment she had slipped her small arms around his neck and whispered his name as he bent to kiss her cheek. Then, unable to stay serious for long, he treated Sophie to a dry-witted rendition of Martin's and Louise's romance while at college in Cambridge.

When she asked him to describe Louise he had said 'fairish and quietish', a description which had already sprung to mind when she had spoken to Louise on the phone, attracted instantly by the soft cadence of her voice.

Sophie realised Luke was staring at her across the table. He had stopped talking and his blue eyes held hers for a moment before he spoke. 'Sophie, I called in at the estate agents on my way home this morning. There's a property they think might be suitable. It's vacant possession. Sounds OK. How do you feel about coming to see it with me?'

'A property?' Her voice seemed to come from someone else a long way off, not her.

He nodded. 'I can't stay here indefinitely, Sophie. People will talk.'

'I don't care,' she protested, her heart thudding against her ribs. 'I don't care what people think any more.'

He looked at her for a long while, arching a doubtful eyebrow. 'You know you don't mean that. And, besides, I care for you.'

Sophie leant forward, wanting to touch him, knowing at this point that she couldn't without making a fool of herself. Holding herself back, she placed her hands flat in her lap. 'You don't know what this property is like. It might be a heap.'

He grinned. 'It might well be. That's why I'd like you to see it. I don't want you thinking I'm leaving to live in a squat.'

No, you just want to leave, she thought in despair; I'm not enough for you — or I'm too much. Either way, I'm losing you.

'Let's see a smile,' he teased her, reaching across the table to lift her chin.

She didn't want to think about it now. She couldn't think about it. Besides, overnight the house might vanish off the face of the earth. Miracles could happen.

'Let's go to bed,' she heard herself suggest as her voice locked in her throat.

'Propositioning me again,' he whispered and, taking her hands, he lifted her to her feet.

★　★　★

The house was far more beautiful than she had expected. Set in its own leafy grounds, it was hidden from view by a crescent of chestnut trees.

'What do you think?' Luke asked as he stood with her looking at the place. Built at the turn of the century, it had picturesque windows overlooking the peaceful garden. The red-brick exterior was newly rendered, and inside each of the spacious rooms was freshly decorated.

Sophie stood in the south-facing reception-room and stared admiringly at the apple-green ceiling, following its graceful curve to the trompe l'oeil archway.

'Well, what do you think?' he asked eagerly, looking out from one of the long windows to the glistening green lawns.

'To be perfectly honest, I didn't realise there were such lovely properties still to be found.'

'Nor did I.' He gave a wry smile. 'Perhaps I hadn't looked hard enough.'

She felt a pang of disappointment; despite her need to find fault with the house, there was none. Picking up from the mantlepiece the papers the estate agent had given Luke, she studied the details. Catching sight of the bold-faced figures at the bottom of the sheet, she was shocked at the high sum involved.

'Phew!' she sighed breathlessly and, looking up to see him watching her, raised her eyebrows. 'Some place!'

He shrugged, coming towards her to take the papers from her hand, throwing them to the ground. 'I like the idea of all the different rooms — we can make love in every one of them; matter of fact, we've probably time to do a test run . . . '

She shook her head slowly, managing a smile. 'Do you never think of anything else?'

'Not when you're around.'

'You know, this is a big house,' she murmured hesitantly, 'a family house. I wouldn't have thought it was quite your style.'

He jerked her around, playfully shaking her. 'You've got a cheek, young lady. Are you insulting my taste?'

She grinned. 'No . . . but you have to admit a penthouse or a converted barn or a really luxurious bachelor pad would be more appropriate.'

'For what?' he growled, pretending to be insulted. 'I've had enough of clinical interiors and computerised kitchens. I want a place of . . . character. I want somewhere I can call home.'

She bit her bottom lip, lifting her eyes slowly. 'Then you want to extend our three-month contract? You're really thinking of staying?'

He looked at her with reproving blue eyes. 'Need you ask that?'

She shrugged, her hands lingering on his broad shoulders as she felt with the familiar increase of pulse-rate the solid muscle and strength beneath her fingers. 'You're considering this place, so I suppose . . . no, I needn't really . . . '

He slid his hands along the small of

her back and up to her hair, pushing them into the softness, bringing her head forward to stare into her eyes. 'You silly girl. Don't you know I've become part of the practice by now? And it's become part of me. Besides which, the young lady who is my partner in crime is also my partner in bed and she is a very worthwhile incentive to stay.'

Oddly the compliment left her cold. It made her feel she was just that to him, a partner, a convenient one, someone with whom he had a perfect arrangement, professionally and per- sonally, a partnership which removed him from the responsibility of caring for someone deeply, allowing him the best of both worlds, perfect freedom emo- tionally and physically.

'A man has to think ahead, to plan, to see what he wants in his mind's eye . . . ' He kissed her again, sliding his hands down over her arms, and, unaware of her thoughts, ambled to the long picture window, where he stared out. 'It's beautiful here. I like the atmosphere, the tranquillity, and the extra room will allow me to have Pip and Louise and Martin to stay. Especially Pip. I'd like her to come in the holidays, give Louise a break and perhaps teach her to ride. She's always wanted a pony. I think maybe I could put one at the back, in the orchard; with proper fencing it would make an excellent paddock . . . what do you think?'

Sophie felt the crashing of her heart, hating herself for the jealousy that erupted inside her. But she couldn't help it. Pip and Louise . . . his surrogate family. Of course, why hadn't she realised? It was so easy to borrow other people's families, then hand them back without having any of the responsibility of committed love and affection. He would go on through life in just that way. Unable to make any lasting commitment, he would neither seek promises nor give them, content to live life as he had always known it, devoid of real love.

A chill ran over her, making her shiver. She had thought she could change him — every woman's mistake. But she was wrong. So terribly wrong.

The light dappled in from the chestnut trees in full bloom outside, sun dropped speckles in a shaft of light as he walked through it, moving over the floor with a soft tread, his long body attired in casual fawn trousers and sweater, enhancing the smouldering blue of his eyes. 'You approve of the house, I take it?' he asked, turning with a smile as though he had just realised she was there.

Sophie shook her head, realising that he had not brought her here for approval; he'd made his mind up long before. 'I'm not going to live in it, Luke, you are. You will have to make your own decision.'

He frowned at her, his broad shoulders silhouetted by the light, a sudden chill in the room — or was it, she wondered desperately, a chill between them?

Walking towards her to lift a strand of blonde hair which had fallen across her cheek, he drew it gently behind her ear, his fingers brushing the soft skin of her cheek, and she inhaled sharply.

'But I want you to like it too,' he said softly. His voice melted her as his fingers lingered on her cheek. 'I've planned for somewhere like this all my life. I want security, a base, roots. Does that seem so wrong to you? I sense your disapproval . . . and I'm not sure why. I should hate you to think badly of me, Sophie — and somehow I get the impression you do.'

She froze into silence. Her heart felt as though it had been pierced with a sword as he left out the one word that made a house a home and that neither money nor position would ever bring.

Love.

Without love, nothing else was of any importance. Her parents had taught her to give love and be loved in return, and she had found a love with Michael and was grateful for it. But for Luke this house would always be a shell, because he would not put love in it.

'I hope you will be happy here,' she said gently, meaning every word, yearning to say the things that she knew she would never be able to say. That she must keep locked in her heart until this mindless passion burnt itself out and she could get on with her life again.

Despite what she now consciously knew, her heart was no longer her own, hadn't been from the first day he had walked into her life.

9

Sophie contented herself with the situation, knowing that she was powerless to do anything about it. Luke wanted the house. He insisted he was unwilling to compromise her any more by living under the same roof indefinitely.

Maybe it didn't look good, but she had told him the truth when she had said she didn't care, even if he chose not to believe her. Not that her protests mattered any more. Luke spent the next afternoon in Cranthorpe tying up the details of the house. The owners wanted a quick sale because they were moving abroad, which couldn't have delighted him more.

It was the end of June. The three-month trial period was almost over and everyone, it seemed, was happy. It should have been a time to celebrate, Sophie thought as, on the following Monday morning she picked up the phone to hear Patricia De Vere's voice.

'I'll get Luke for you,' Sophie answered briskly and hailed Luke before he attended to his next client.

Ten minutes later he stuck his head around her door. 'I told Trish we'd be along tomorrow afternoon.'

'We?' Sophie frowned, looking up from her desk.

'You're coming with me, aren't you?'

Sophie hesitated, on the point of saying she would be too busy, when the whole situation struck her as ridiculous. Patricia De Vere couldn't eat her! What in heaven's name was she afraid of?

'Why not?' she shrugged with a brave smile.

Did he look a little surprised? she wondered.

But then, with a broad grin, he winked at her. 'Right, then, it's a date.'

★　★　★

She realised their lovemaking had changed quite subtly. Something, she decided, must have happened in Cambridge. Or perhaps he was now just eager to leave, a thought she thrust firmly away, reluctant to admit there was a distinct possibility it might be true.

She, on the other hand, having missed him so much, had never felt so comfortable with her feelings, abandoning all inhibitions and guilt which had, at first, made her ashamed of her responses. Now she felt like the proverbial candy-store owner who was at liberty to dip in and eat any of his goods whenever he liked.

That evening, though, self-control seemed furthest from his mind as he pulled her into his arms and kissed her hungrily.

'Wh . . . what was that for?' she stammered as she gazed at him curiously.

He shrugged, his blue eyes softly melting over her face. 'I needed you . . . badly.'

She laughed softly. 'You're funny!'

'Funny ha-ha?'

She shook her head. 'No, just . . . well, I can't explain it.' She paused, running her fingers along the hard ridge of his shoulder, uncertain whether she should voice her doubts. Sometimes she felt like a possessive, scheming mistress. Sometimes she felt like a spurned lover, though he always took the greatest care to please her. It was odd. She just didn't understand what was happening between them any more. Perhaps it was because she had become desperate for his love. Yet she knew he would never say those words . . .

'Is there anything worrying you?' she asked softly, gazing into his eyes, searching them.

'Like what?' he asked, frowning.

She shrugged. 'I thought maybe Pip — or the house. You just seem preoccupied, a little distanced.'

Resorting to his usual line of defence — humour — he grinned. 'Nothing a few hours of one-to-one counselling won't cure. Would you like to be my therapist?'

She narrowed her eyes. 'And dig around in that cauldron of a mind of yours? No, thank you.'

'It's not my mind I'm worried about,' he whispered, kissing her. 'It's this tired and weary body which needs a little attention — ' He kissed her again, his lips moving over hers so seductively that, before she knew what was happening, the subject had been neatly avoided and intuition alerted her to the fact that to try to discuss anything with him tonight would only end in frustration.

Then came a sweet and savage plundering of her lips as he began to tug the white blouse from her skirt, his hands travelling up underneath it to seek out her heated flesh, pulling her firmly against him as his hard arousal caused her to groan and thrust her hands deeply into his hair.

His mouth covered her neck in slow sensual kisses and tiny bites, desire running like a forest fire beneath her skin. She no longer cared about conversation, no longer cared about anything, save for the need deep inside her which had to be assuaged in the only way she knew how.

★ ★ ★

The reasons why she had agreed to visit Longhaven now escaped her as she sat beside Luke in the Jaguar, staring up at the green archway of trees above, fingers of light piercing the thick branches to fall delicately on the road ahead.

Luke nodded to two women working in a field before the main entrance. 'Longhaven is self-sufficient,' he explained as they drove past and into the winding drive that led up to the house. 'Each of Trish's house guests contributes while they are 'resting'. She has a gardener who lives in a cottage nearby and comes in to help grow the veg.'

Sophie smiled wryly. 'I wouldn't have

thought Trish was green.'

Luke laughed. 'No, but a lot of her guests are. Appearances can be deceiving.'

A sentiment which she wholeheartedly agreed with as Luke jammed on the brakes outside the sprawling ivy-covered house.

'Luke, darling!' The actress appeared from out of nowhere, embracing him as he climbed from the car. 'And Sophie,' she added, her voice lowering. 'How sweet of you to come.'

Patricia wore diaphanous rainbow-coloured robes and rows of coloured hippy beads, a role, Sophie decided, which did not sit well on her sophisticated shoulders. She waved a slender hand. 'Come along and I'll show you the house.'

Luke seemed not to notice as she slid a hand through his arm and left Sophie to follow them.

'These are my house guests,' she introduced as several people stopped to talk, in no time at all describing their many appearances on tour or in the West End theatres.

The house had many rooms, mostly cluttered with theatre memorabilia, and they were shown each one, Luke seeming to know his way around as they went from ground floor to the tiny Victorian attic rooms at the top of the house.

'Now to the stables,' Patricia announced as they trod the creaky staircase down to the front door. Sophie noticed that two of the women, the girls from the fields, had changed into jodhpurs, and they accompanied them across a court-yard to the stables.

One by one they passed the occupied boxes, Patricia explaining that her guests often stabled and grazed their horses at Longhaven. At the last box a conker-brown horse put its head over the stable door marked 'India'.

'She's lovely, isn't she?' Patricia said proudly. 'Half Arab stallion with a French Anglo-Arab mother.'

'Beautiful,' Sophie agreed as she

stroked the soft satiny head and pert ears. 'How old is she?'

'Six,' Patricia said as she unbolted the bottom half of the door and opened it, flicking up her dark gaze to meet Luke's. 'She's of great sentimental value to me. Didn't Luke tell you? I bought her on the day Luke and I met at a Paris thoroughbred sale five years ago.'

Sophie realised no answer was necessary as Patricia walked in, going straight to the horse and showing Luke the bandaged leg. Sophie felt the breath leave her body, but she managed to look outwardly unmoved, her heart racing as she heard Luke and Patricia discussing the injury.

Had Luke met Patricia while she was still married? she wondered. Lost in thought, it was a few minutes before she realised Luke was speaking as he unwound the bandage.

'Who applied this bandage?' he asked Patricia sharply, running his fingers over the leg.

Patricia shrugged. 'The local vet. He said it was a sprain — but his bandage came off and one of the girls reapplied it. I can't remember who.'

'You should have called him in again.' Luke glanced up with a frown. 'Whoever bandaged India's leg made it too tight, which hasn't helped her recovery.'

Patricia sighed. 'How annoying. I was hoping you might be able to suggest something, Luke, darling, that might have her well for the Cranthorpe show in July.'

Luke's face darkened. He opened his case and took out a fresh elastic bandage. 'The last thing I would worry about is showing her, Trish!'

Sophie noticed that the actress looked annoyed, little red dots appearing on her cheeks. 'Is there nothing you can do? An injection or something?' she persisted impatiently.

Luke shook his head as he began to snip away the unsatisfactory tape. 'What I can do is to bandage both legs,

251

since by her posture I can see she is taking more weight on the sound leg than the injured one.'

Sophie bent beside him and helped with the discarded cloth, her eyes coming up to meet his as the space beneath it revealed an unpleasant swelling. Holding the tip of the bandage for him at the knee, Luke gently unrolled the rest to follow the natural contour of the leg, checking to see that the completed work did not interfere with the mobility of the fetlock joint.

'You've had X-rays?' he asked as he rubbed his chin.

'Yes; nothing showed up, apparently,' Patricia dismissed coolly.

'Then it's a case of rest, as I'm sure your vet told you. See how she goes over the next few days. There's nothing there which shouldn't heal naturally. If, by the end of next week, she's no better, you must call him back in. If there are any injections to be given then he is the one to give them.'

'Why can't you? Surely this once — '

Luke shook his head. 'India isn't my patient and I don't intend poaching, Trish. Your man was working on the theory of a simple sprain and it would have improved by now if someone had not interfered with the bandage.'

'What a wretched nuisance,' Patricia sighed, her dark eyes annoyed.

'It would be — if she went permanently lame,' Luke admonished, snapping shut his case, standing up to run his hand over India's glossy back. 'You'll have to wait to show her until next year,' he muttered, 'and that's an end to it, I'm afraid.'

As a tense silence descended Sophie watched Patricia's face. She soon had a smile on it and as they walked from the box she asked pleasantly, 'Stay for tea, do. Strawberries from our own garden.'

'Sounds tempting,' Luke grinned and glanced at Sophie.

'Oh, yes, fine,' Sophie agreed, dying a million deaths as Patricia clung to Luke's arm as they walked back, making her glance surreptitiously at her watch, checking off the slowly passing minutes that seemed to stretch endlessly until it was time to leave.

Patricia De Vere's tea consisted of luscious strawberries coated in thick cream, glistening with white sugar.

The buffet was a communal affair, a balancing of plates on knees, and non-stop talk of the theatre, a living, breathing addiction, it seemed, even when people weren't working in it.

Sophie listened distractedly to her companion's chatter, a young woman who had appeared on a TV commercial. As she listened Sophie's attention strayed across the room to the tall form of Luke leaning against a wall, talking to Patricia.

Heart aching, she turned away. The pang of jealousy was like a knife twisting in her ribs. They looked so deep in conversation. She willed him to look across the room and smile, but his face was turned down, intent on the actress.

By the time the girl had stopped

talking and moved away, Sophie was beset by doubts. Why, after all, had Patricia invited her out here if not to illustrate the fact she and Luke were still on intimate terms?

India was already being treated by another vet — Luke was not in a position to treat the horse. Everyone who had even a passing knowledge of large animals knew that it was unethical to treat another vet's patient. She could not believe Patricia wasn't aware of this, but had used India as an excuse to bring them out here and drive home the point that she and Luke were still involved.

'Ready to go?'

Sophie blinked, staring up into Luke's smiling face.

'You look as though you were in another world.'

She blushed. 'Do I?' She felt his hand slide behind her as he perched on the arm of the chair she was sitting in.

'You look bored to tears, to tell you the truth.'

She sighed, her eyes going around the room for her companion who had been talking about her TV ad. 'The poor girl. She was telling me how they made commercials and videos, but I'm afraid I lost track.'

He laughed, his hand gently playing in her hair. 'She probably didn't even notice as long as she had an audience.' He bent down and whispered in her ear, 'How do you feel about making a break for it?'

'Won't Patricia be upset at our sneaking away?' she asked with a frown.

He chuckled. 'She's on the phone. I don't suppose she'll notice. Apparently it's her agent. She'll be gossiping on the thing for hours.'

Sophie sighed as she studied the bowls of strawberries as yet undevoured. 'As a matter of fact,' she murmured with a wry smile, 'I don't think I can manage another single one.'

'Me neither. Come on, then.' He held out his hand. 'Let's vanish while we can.'

They made their escape unobserved.

The evening was perfect as they drove away from Longhaven. A golden sun dazzled them and they had to flick down the visors to keep the glare from their eyes.

The countryside, ablaze with colour, was noisy with summer birdsong, and, with the windows down, a warm breeze blew in.

Luke's forearm rested on the open window, his shirtsleeves turned up, the glint of his gold watch magnified in the sun. She noticed how deliciously strong and firm his brown wrists were, how his long fingers gripped the wheel and little black hairs sprang out from the open-necked shirt, free from the chest muscle beneath.

They travelled for an hour, and then in the distance appeared the little hump of woods jutting out from the trees that heralded Cranthorpe. Behind these a spire glinted, from the church of St John's, an historic old building that was crammed each year with summer visitors. Then, as the car moved on, the practice conicals appeared, one by one, set against the buttery gold of the evening sky.

'Home sweet home,' Luke murmured and took her hand and squeezed it, lifting it to his lips and brushing a kiss there.

Sophie felt the terrible pang again. She wanted to ask outright about Patricia. She wanted to know and yet she didn't have the courage to ask, for one reason only — for fear of the answer.

'You're very quiet,' he murmured, glancing at her with a frown.

She smiled, lifting her shoulders carelessly. 'Enjoying the ride, that's all.'

He grinned. 'Tell you what, I'll drop you off at the house and then buy a take-away and a bottle of Cranthorpe's best vino and we'll make a day of it.'

She nodded, smiling. 'That sounds nice.'

'Settled, then.' He frowned back at the road, whistling.

Sophie bit down on her lip as she felt the ridiculous urge to ask him to stop the car and just talk with her. She wanted to tell him she loved him, yet she knew those were the words he did not want to hear.

Instead she took a breath. 'I'll ring over to the girls and let them know we're back.'

'I need a hug first,' he whispered as he halted the car at the house and leaned across to unclip her safety belt.

He pulled her towards him, his lips brushing hers in the lightest caress. 'In fact, I need more than that.'

She pulled his head down, her fingers running up into the thick dark hair. Kissing him, she felt all her doubts dissolve as they always did when she was lost in his arms.

'I get the distinct impression you've been miles away today, somewhere where I can't reach you,' he said softly, staring into her eyes.

She put her hand up to his face. 'I'm here,' she murmured. 'Kiss me again.'

He kissed her again, deeply and longingly, a kiss which made her drag in a deep breath as he slowly drew away.

'We could have eggs again,' he muttered throatily, 'and forget the Chinese.'

Sophie laughed and pushed him away. 'Go fetch your take-away . . . I'll be waiting.'

He grinned. 'You'd better be!'

The house was silent as she let herself in, but for Steamer's exultant welcome and his barking as she opened the kitchen door for him to run through to the garden.

Restless, she wandered into the garden too, where the hazy sun turned the evening greens to silvery grey, scents of the flowers filling the air with a potent sweetness.

Perhaps she would ask Luke about Patricia tonight. After a meal and a glass of wine as they relaxed. She might enquire about Paris . . . after all, it was natural enough to be curious. The unspoken vow not to encroach on each other's territory would surely bend after today's visit to Longhaven?

Suddenly Steamer barked from the house and Sophie's attention flew to the interlocking gate. Luke couldn't have returned so quickly.

'Who's there?' she called as she hurried across the lawn, peering through the lattice to see who it was. Her heart sank as with a shock she saw it was Hamish Burns.

'Sophie?' He smiled as she warily slid the bolt and opened the gate a few inches.

'Hamish, what brings you this way?' she asked hesitantly.

'I came to say goodbye, actually. I've resigned from Hadleys Pharmaceuticals.'

She realised she had allowed him to walk past her and through into the garden.

'I had no idea.' She hesitated before closing the gate and, on impulse, left it slightly open. Steamer barked at his feet furiously. Obviously this was one visitor he did not like.

She told the dog to lie down and then frowned at Hamish. 'I'm sorry you're leaving, Hamish. You've always been most helpful to us — '

'You've not been an easy lady to find,' he interrupted rudely as he sat, uninvited, in one of the garden chairs. 'I called at the surgery and the girls said you'd taken the afternoon off. Then I happened to see your . . . guest drive off and thought this would be a good chance to catch you alone.'

Sophie felt a sudden chill as she stared into his narrowed blue eyes. 'Luke will be back soon,' she said uneasily.

'Are you still involved with him?' He stared up at her accusingly and Sophie gasped, her hands clenching at her sides.

'It's none of your business, Hamish. If you've come here to be offensive then I'm afraid you've wasted your time. Please leave.'

'So . . . you are!' He gave a bitter laugh, getting to his feet and grabbing hold of her arm. 'Didn't you pay any attention to the warning I gave you?'

Sophie gasped. 'Let go of me, Hamish.'

Steamer sprang up, growling.

'Stop — !' Sophie began, her words dying in her throat as he jerked her closer.

'You didn't give us a chance,' he muttered as she froze, her body seeming to lock where she stood. 'Sophie, don't you see . . . you and I — ?'

'Hamish, please let me go!' She managed to bring up her hands and push against his chest, but he was so strong that her protest died on her lips.

He cursed the dog snapping at his heels and lashed out viciously with his foot.

'Hamish — don't!' Sophie cried out as she heard Steamer yelp.

But her aggressor's face was distorted with rage as he turned back. Real fear gripped her as she stared into it.

'Sophie, don't you know how I feel about you?' he muttered, pulling her against him, his flushed face pushed up against her own.

She gasped as his hold tightened and his fingers bit into her skin. Then somehow his body seemed to be lifting off her, flying backwards, hurtling across the lawn until finally he knocked into a chair and toppled over, the shock evident on his astounded face.

Above him stood Luke. 'Get up,' he growled and gave him a helping hand on the back of his collar, thrusting him towards the gate with a forceful shove.

Hamish stumbled, his face crimson, cursing as he went.

'You're on private property,' Luke stormed, his face dark with anger. 'Get out — or be thrown out.'

Sophie watched, mesmerised, heart pounding, as Hamish hesitated. But it was obvious he was no match for Luke's strength, and with a final curse over his shoulder he slouched back through the gate. Following him, Luke made sure of his departure.

Sophie began to regain her composure, taking a long, deep breath and calling a bewildered Steamer over. He was such a placid dog. He'd never gone for anyone in his life, had never needed to. She sank to her knees and hugged him as he licked her, wagging his tail ferociously.

'What the hell was that all about?' Luke bent down to ease her up from the ground, his big hands supporting her arms. 'Did he hurt you?'

She shook her head, trying to smile, but she had begun to shake. 'No, he didn't hurt me. He came to tell me he wasn't working for the drug house any longer.'

'Strange way of conveying a message,' he grated, pushing back her hair from her forehead, searching her eyes. 'Are you sure you're OK? You're trembling like a leaf.'

Sophie nodded, collapsing into his arms. 'He just lost his temper.'

'But why come here to lose it?' Luke peeled her away, staring at her with a confused frown.

She shook her head, casting her eyes downward.

'Come in,' Luke said gently, taking her arm, twisting her towards the kitchen door. 'You need a drink.'

A little later she sat on the sofa and sniffed the drink Luke had poured her — a tiny measure of brandy. She sipped it, wrinkling her nose.

'Drink it up. Medicinal,' he grinned.

She did as she was told, the white heat burning her throat as it slipped down.

'Better?' He sat beside her, taking her hands.

She suddenly remembered the vicious kick and called Steamer. He padded in, ears forlornly drooping. 'Hamish kicked him, Luke. Do you think you could have a look at him?'

Luke nodded, going down on his knees, carefully rolling Steamer onto his back, checking his ribcage and then his limbs. Playfully ruffling his collar and running his fingers over his head and jaw, Luke patted him. 'You're OK, aren't you, boy?' he said as he sat by Sophie. 'Why did he kick

266

the dog?' he asked gravely.

Sophie sighed, sitting back, resting her head against the cushions. 'Because he was protecting me. Hamish misinterpreted my reasons for going out with him. I told him to go. He wouldn't — ' She stopped, staring down at the empty brandy glass. 'Now you're going to say 'I told you so',' she sighed again, unable to look at him.

He tipped up her chin, clucking his tongue. 'I leave you alone for five minutes and look what happens.' He regarded her steadily and then slipped his arms around her to give her a hug, drawing her head down on his chest as she sank unresistingly into his warm strength. 'I think the guy is jealous as hell,' he said softly, touching her hair with featherlight strokes.

She closed her eyes, breathing in his scent. What if Luke hadn't come back when he did? she wondered helplessly. The same thought, she realised, must have occurred to him, as he chuckled. 'When I got in the off-licence I went to pay for the wine and realised I must have left my wallet here when I changed my clothes at lunchtime. Needless to say, they whipped back the bottle, not at all convinced by so pathetic a story.'

Sophie laughed as she visualised the scene. 'So we've nothing to eat — and nothing to drink?'

'Not a bean, not a thimbleful.'

She shrugged. 'I don't much care.' The brandy was gradually making its warm way down to her toes.

'Brave words,' he mocked, pulling her into his arms.

She felt brave enough now but she hadn't forgotten how she had felt with Hamish. 'To be honest, I was terrified in the garden,' she admitted, shuddering at the memory of Hamish's face pressed into hers and his hands roughly shaking her.

He frowned as he kissed her flushed cheeks. 'Don't worry, if he shows up again I'll call the police.'

Her lips opened in surprise. 'I don't think he would dare!'

His eyes became shuttered. 'You're too trusting. I'm worried for you, Sophie.'

She shook her head with more confidence than she felt. 'Don't be.'

He paused. 'I shan't always be around . . . ' he reminded her bluntly.

She nodded, understanding, her heart aching at the thought.

Then his mouth twisted into a crooked smile. 'Well, I'm certainly not leaving you alone here this evening. We either go out to eat, raid the freezer, or, dare I say it, scramble eggs?'

She nuzzled her face into the warmth of his neck. 'I'm not sure I've much appetite at the moment.'

He ran his hands over her back feeling the indentation of her spine with delicate, caressing strokes. 'Me neither.'

She stared up into his dark, brooding face. All the questions she had planned to ask him were slipping around in her mind. But when he kissed her again she forgot them all.

10

Hannah grazed with her foal in the small paddock behind the house.

Sophie and her mother could see the two men from where they stood in the kitchen, Luke on his haunches examining Jake and her father watching.

'Jake's feeding well?' Sophie asked as she gazed out, tea-towel in one hand, cup in the other, her eye following the familiar line of Luke's broad shoulders as he moved.

Anne Edmonds noted the expression in her daughter's eyes. She closed the fridge door, going to stand beside her. 'Well enough. Hannah seems to be able to provide him with sufficient milk, but your father would be out there watching them at midnight if I let him.'

Sophie laughed. 'Poor Dad. Hannah's pregnancy has been quite a trauma for him.'

Anne nodded. 'To be honest I don't remember him getting so worked up about you or your brother's births. If I didn't know him better I'd say he was in post-natal shock.'

Both women burst out laughing. Sophie knew Hannah meant the world to her father. Sophie's gaze went back to the scene outside. 'I'm glad everything turned out all right. Michael was so sure Hannah shouldn't foal again.'

Anne paused, her eyes thoughtful as she watched her daughter. 'Do you know, darling, that's the first time in two years that you've spoken naturally about Michael? We've always been half afraid to bring the subject up.'

Sophie turned, her expression startled as colour flooded her cheeks. 'I . . . I didn't even think about it . . . '

Anne slipped her hand into her daughter's, squeezing it. 'That's remarkable in itself, don't you think?'

Sophie nodded slowly. 'Yes, I suppose so.'

After a brief pause Anne asked, 'Is it Luke?'

Sophie's brown eyes widened. 'No! I — ' She shook her head, her heart racing as she knew it was impossible to lie to her mother.

'I thought it might be,' Anne said gently.

Sophie lowered her eyes to the cup she was holding. 'I don't think anything can come of it. I know how I feel. But I don't think Luke could ever feel more than . . . ' She shrugged, suddenly aware that a lump had formed in her throat.

'May I offer you one small piece of advice, Sophie?' her mother asked hesitantly, squeezing her hand again. 'Without you thinking of me as an interfering old busybody?'

Sophie looked up. Her eyes were warm as she gazed at her mother. 'You've never interfered in my life, Mum, you or Dad. I've always loved you both very much for that.'

Anne smiled. After a while she

ventured, 'I can see Luke thinks a great deal of you. But under the circumstances — at the house . . . you're not giving yourselves a chance.'

Sophie frowned, shaking her head. 'I don't understand.'

'The house was Michael,' her mother said simply. 'His creation, an extension of his persona. Don't misunderstand me, it's a beautiful place, but essentially it's all Michael's character. I think Luke is too much of a man to be able to ignore Michael's stamp. I'm sure he can cope with the practice, for that was equally Michael, but other people share the space there — Howard, John, the girls and you, of course. But your home is another matter . . . '

Sophie frowned. 'I . . . I hadn't thought of it like that. You may be right. But, anyway, it's too late to worry. he's found a property just outside of town. He's moving out next week.'

Anne hesitated. 'You'll miss him, Sophie.'

She nodded. 'I shall. I never thought

I would. In fact, I dreaded him coming to stay. After Michael — '

'You spent far too long feeling guilty over his death, darling. Your father and I could see it, but we couldn't get through to you. Luke came along at the right time in your life. Be thankful for that, whatever happens.'

Sophie stared at her mother. Suddenly she realised how difficult it must have been for her parents, unable to penetrate the cocoon she had built around herself. She saw it all quite plainly now, but only because her feelings towards Luke had helped her face the truth.

'They're coming in,' Anne said, discreetly moving away from the window, removing the cup from Sophie's hand. 'Don't worry, everything will work out,' she added quietly. 'Luke has been an enriching experience in your life. You can only go forward from now.'

Sophie held her mother's hands briefly, then hugged her. 'I love you,

Mum,' she murmured, moving away as the men's voices could be heard coming along the passageway.

As Sophie helped her mother set the tea on the huge pine table she felt a deep pang of gratefulness wash over her at her mother's words. Michael would always occupy a special place in her heart. But their marriage had not been perfect. Michael had never wanted a family. His refusal would have always been a major stumbling block. Now she could admit that the months before his death had been drainingly unhappy as the subject had become like a wedge, driven deep into the heart of their marriage.

As she looked up and Luke entered the kitchen with her father, seeing his face gave her heart a twist. Perhaps he had felt uncomfortable at the house, but had never mentioned it? Perhaps that was the reason he wanted to move as quickly as he could? Had she been reading more into the situation than was there?

He smiled at her, his blue eyes amethyst under their hoods, and her heart leapt. He wore a grey shirt and grey cords, his deep tan giving him a Mediterranean appearance, the sun having darkened the grainy skin to a perfect velvety brown, whereas hers was a light golden colour, her fairness a complete opposite as they stood beside one another.

Ralph Edmonds nodded to the picture through the kitchen window. 'Just look at them,' he grinned.

They all turned to see Jake trying to skit around his mother, his long legs clumsily getting in the way.

'The foal slip around his head will simplify breaking,' Luke said as they sat down. 'And I'll give him his first anti-tetanus soon. Other than that it's just a question of letting him exercise for growth and muscle development.'

Ralph nodded, thrusting a hand through his grey hair as he stretched up from the table to observe his horses again.

Anne pushed his shoulder. 'Eat, Ralph!'

Everyone laughed and Sophie caught Luke's eye, realising how at ease he was with her family. Michael, though he was a good son-in-law, had rarely had time to talk to her parents. In fact, it occurred to her now that he had never sat in this kitchen, never laughed as they were laughing now. Luke had brought fun and laughter to her life.

The conversation drifted on, mainly about horses. The tea eaten and the foal checked for the last time, they bade her parents goodbye, Sophie giving her mother a last hug.

The sun streamed in through the Jaguar's windows and Luke turned to her with a soft smile. 'Jake's going to be quite something.'

She nodded. 'Dad's intention is to start a completely new line of Anglo-Arabs. He just can't believe he's got what he's wanted for so long and never thought, until you safely delivered Jake, he would ever get.'

Luke stretched a hand across and covered her own small one. 'He deserves to succeed.'

She shivered, loving the feel of his hand on the rough material of her jodhpurs. While he had been doing the examinations of Hannah and Jake she had taken the opportunity to ride one of her father's horses. The ride had been refreshing and she only wished Luke could have ridden with her. She realised she wanted to experience everything with him, wanted to know what he felt and what he thought. She wanted to share. It was beginning to be like a hunger she could not satisfy.

Looking down as she flicked through her notebook, chewing on her lip, she studied Chas Bell's name.

'We aren't far from the Bells' place,' she murmured, trying hard to get her concentration back. 'I see you've a visit for this week. Why don't we call?'

'I can't take you to a pig farm,' he protested with a wry smile. 'Not in those things. You look too sexy in

278

jodhpurs to get messed up.'

She giggled. 'Is it Chas's sow again, the one who had her head stuck and you bathed in washing-up liquid?'

Luke laughed. 'No, just an iron injection for her piglets, make sure they aren't anaemic. So, unless I meet nose-on with their mother, you needn't get your hopes up of seeing me mud-wrestling.'

'Pity. I quite fancy that.' She cast him a sideways grin.

Luke raised his eyebrows. 'So do I, but not with a pig.'

'Now who's being a spoilsport!'

Luke swerved the Jaguar into a lay-by. 'I'll show you just how much of a spoilsport I am . . . ' Jerking on the brakes, he pulled her to him, unclipping her belt as she fought him, her laughter echoing as they tumbled around, her head lifting in a wild mix of playfulness and surrender as he tried to kiss her. She felt her head swim as his hands plundered her hair and brought her face to his, his mouth touching and tasting with teasing little kisses, as he held her wrists, forcing her to be still.

Then suddenly they were both silent and his lips found hers in a deeply passionate kiss, his hands going over her body, bringing her to him with unexpected force.

As he kissed her a strong desire welled up in her and she had to bite back the words that were desperate to escape from her throbbing lips. She longed for a sign that she occupied some corner of his heart, that this was not just a physical affair. She prayed he would say something, anything, to make her feel her love was reciprocated.

Burning with her need, she felt his hands on her body. Strong, sinewy muscle moved under the grey shirt beneath her fingertips. Their playful interaction left her unable to control her need and it rose up in her as his sweet tongue plundered her mouth and every sense was sent crashing around in her body, her desire all-consuming, until she pushed breathlessly away.

'I love you,' she breathed, losing her long-fought battle to keep silent. 'I love you, Luke.'

Their eyes met.

Her heart pounded until she thought it would jump out of her chest. A car swished by outside. Somewhere in the distance a plane droned, high above them. The beauty of an English summertime was woven around them. And in his eyes she saw despair.

'Sophie . . . ' He gently reached up and laid a finger on her lips. 'Don't.'

Her voice was thick as she spoke. 'I can't help the way I feel. Luke, it's just not possible for me to be — casually involved . . . '

He let her go, gently clipping back her seat-belt with a deep sigh. For a moment he was quiet. 'Sophie, I thought I — '

She turned her head to the window, a terrible ache of humiliation inside her. 'You don't have to feel the same way. I don't expect you to.'

He pulled her around. 'You don't

understand . . . '

'I do!'

He starred at her, frowning. 'Sophie, try to get things into perspective. You were a married woman and you loved Michael. And I'm not Michael.'

She looked at him in shock. 'Is that what you think?'

'It wouldn't work.' He shrugged as he sat there, the sun shining in on his dark features. 'We knew that from the beginning, didn't we? Neither of us wanted more than we could give.'

'Luke, I shall always be grateful — '

'Which is exactly what you feel. Gratitude. Not love,' he emphasised firmly.

She took a deep breath, her heart pounding again. 'Don't tell me what I feel, Luke,' she said in a low voice, hurt to the quick. 'I know how I feel, but I'm sorry if expressing my feelings has displeased you. I can see I shouldn't have said it.'

He shook his head, lifting his shoulders. 'Sophie, I thought what we had between us was good for us both.'

Her face paled. 'Do you know you're talking in the past tense?'

He looked away. 'Just a figure of speech.'

'Do you want to end it . . . us?' She could hardly believe she had asked.

He brought his face around to stare at her. 'Do you?'

She shook her head. 'No, I don't. At least . . . not yet.'

He nodded, his blue eyes suddenly soft. 'Sophie, I don't want to hurt you. I'd hoped I'd made it plain who I was — and what I was.'

She sighed. He had. 'You are a confirmed bachelor. You are my practice partner. And you are a . . . temporary lover.'

He leaned across and lifted her head in his hands. 'Don't do this,' he whispered on a groan.

She melted at his touch, she loved him so much. And yet it had been her biggest mistake in saying it. She folded her hands over his and nodded slowly in obedience.

'You leave in two weeks,' she breathed on a deep sigh. 'Let's leave it at that.'

Sophie knew that if she let him kiss her she would burst into tears. Making a last effort, she smiled. He let go of her face, drawing his fingers slowly away from her hot cheeks.

'Let's go to Chas's,' she said, her voice, miraculously, intact.

He nodded, clipping his belt back in, starting up the engine. Sophie stared at his profile. She could read nothing in it, but she knew with a sinking heart it was the beginning of the end. She had to let him go.

They had just two weeks left.

★   ★   ★

Luke began to tie a rope halter around the smallest of Pete Arnott's calves. Reducing the big loop so the knot was under the calf's chin, he drew the loose end over the nose, pulling it back under the rope on the left of the calf's jaw, tying the end to the vertical iron tethering pole with a half-bow.

Sophie, who was watching, saw Peter shift back his cap from his head.

'Dunno what I'm keeping these for. Must be mad,' he groaned and turned to shout at his excited grandchildren outside the shed. 'Go and hose down the yard if you've nothing better to do!'

A little girl with blonde pigtails and very blue eyes stuck her head over the half-door. 'Grandad, can we come and watch?'

'No, you can't,' Pete grumbled. 'The vet don't want an audience — not like you lot. Now go and make yourselves useful.'

Luke looked up from where he was, crouched by the calf. 'How old are they, Pete?'

'Sally's five and Simon's six and a pair of devils they are too. I wanted to send these calves to market and what do you know? They've named 'em Tom and Gerry. Taught them to drink. Calves nearly sucked their little fingers off, but they stuck it out and had them eating calf pencils before you could bat an eyelid. Needless to say, when I had 'em earmarked for market I met with a bit of stiff opposition.'

Luke chuckled and got up, dusting down his green overalls spattered with straw. Sally's blue eyes still glimmered over the door and her grandfather was just about to shout again when Luke stopped him.

'Hello, you two.' He pushed open the half-door.

Two blonde children entered with smiles from ear to ear. Though Simon was older, he was also the smaller. He looked up at Luke and asked, 'What are you going to do? Not . . . ?' his voice trailed.

Luke shook his head. 'I'm not going to hurt them. Tom and Gerry are both male calves. They have to become grown up if they are to live on the farm, as your grandad has allowed.'

Two sets of blue eyes swivelled to their grandad.

Sophie suppressed a smile. They were delightful children. Absolutely filthy, but gorgeous. A hand clutched at her heart and squeezed it as Luke talked to them in his gentle way.

It had been a week since they had talked in the car, and with every passing day she knew it was coming nearer to his moving. Silently, in that moment, their future had been agreed. Her confession had brought, for better or worse, this phase in her life to a natural conclusion and her heart ached more and more with every day.

'After this small op, Tom and Gerry will be called steers, not calves,' Luke said as Sally gazed up into the same colour eyes as her own.

'Does that mean they're grown up?' she asked sensibly.

Luke nodded. 'They will be more placid and easier to handle, otherwise eventually they would become bulls. And you know what bulls are like.'

Simon nudged his sister in the ribs. 'Like Trojan, Grandad's bull in north meadow, who chased us.'

Luke laughed and nodded. 'I'm afraid bulls can't be kept as pets.'

'Nor will these,' Pete Arnott put in briskly. Then as everyone's head swivelled to look at him he relented hesitantly. 'Well, maybe for a year or two perhaps.'

The children looked back to Luke. Sally said, 'You won't hurt them?'

Luke shook his dark head, reaching out to hold her tiny hand. 'No, I have an anaesthetic to help me. No worse for them than going to the dentist for you.'

Sally giggled shyly. Simon's expression was unsure. 'We'd better go and hose down, then,' he said, pulling his sister after him.

Sophie watched the two little figures trudge out of the shed in oversized green wellingtons. Luke had been so gentle with them — like a gentle giant.

'I would let them stay . . . ' Luke hesitated with a shrug. 'But as it's a castration I don't think it's quite the right op for them to witness just yet.'

''Course not,' agreed Pete whole-heartedly, sliding the bolt firmly. 'Can't bring m'self to watch, let alone them. Gives me the willies just thinking about it.'

Luke grinned at Sophie. 'Are we all set?' he asked with a wink.

She nodded, having prepared what was needed on a small portable table at the rear of the shed. She was dressed, too, in protective green overalls and boots. Passing him the swab of antiseptic, she watched his supple figure bend to clean the first calf's scrotum.

Pete Arnott visibly shuddered.

He talked all the way through the procedure, not caring to look, his arm perched on the half-door of the stable. He went into rhapsodies about the ultra-new freeze-branding equipment Luke had brought him, but, Sophie noted, he was not a man who cared to see his male calves castrated.

She passed Luke the filled syringe and he injected local anaesthetic into each testis. The little calf moved, but on the halter Luke had made he remained still as the anaesthetic began to work.

Ten minutes later Luke made the incision through the fragile covering of skin. He withrew all that was necessary and severed the vessels and membranes in a swift, skilful action that took no longer than a few minutes. Finally washing the wound with antiseptic, he moved to the next calf and repeated the operation.

Soon Tom and Gerry looked none the worse for wear, their big brown eyes with their long lashes looking left and right for the children, whom they had come to associate with the food buckets.

Luke slipped the bolt and called to the children. They both came charging in and came to a halt as they stopped by Sophie, scanning the place with their bright blue eyes.

Sophie stroked Gerry's soft head over the small, debudded horn stumps. 'You can give them a cuddle,' she said.

'They're both a bit sleepy, but they're fine.'

The three grown-ups grinned as they stood outside the shed, watching the two children inspect their new steers.

'That's a business I don't much like,' confessed Pete as he walked with them to the Jaguar. 'Been a farmer all my life and still can't get used to it.'

Luke laughed. 'No problem with the little ones, Pete. It's characters like Trojan who worry me.'

Pete shuddered. 'Perish the thought.' He leaned in through the open window as Luke flicked on the starter. 'And thanks for talking to the kids — they're nosy little blighters, but those calves mean the world to them.'

Luke laughed. 'No problem. I just wish all our clients were so easily satisfied. See you, Pete.'

The farmer raised his cap and stood away as Luke reversed from the yard. He jammed on the brakes as Sally and Simon ran past their grandfather, yelling and waving.

Two sets of grubby hands came on the car door and two muddy faces looked in. 'Will you be coming back?' asked Sally, her blue eyes pinned on Luke.

He grinned, nodding. 'I hope so.'

Simon hauled himself up to stare at Sophie. 'Both of you?'

'Maybe,' Sophie smiled. 'Look after Tom and Gerry.'

Luke ruffled Sally's blonde head. 'You'd better get those steers fed, hadn't you?' he chuckled.

The children waved all the way until the Jaguar was out of sight, two small figures in large green wellingtons holding pails almost as big as themselves. Sophie's heart gave a little tug and she sat back in her seat with a sigh.

'Nice kids,' Luke said.

Sophie nodded.

'Being brought up with animals makes a difference.'

'Yes.' She looked down at her hands clenched in her lap. Her mind was a turmoil of thought. Not the least among them was that she was twenty-eight years of age. Even if she had a child now, which was impossible, of course, but if she did she would be thirty-three before it was Sally's age.

Well, even at thirty-three she would be a good mother. She knew a lot about herself now that she hadn't known at twenty-one. Self-discovery was important, a learning and accepting of values that were important to a woman as she grew older. Communication, time, interest, patience — all these she understood better now. She felt she could give so much to a child . . . but what was she doing? She wasn't remotely likely to have a child!

'Broody?' Luke said, catching her drift.

She blushed furiously. 'No!'

'Fibber.' He glanced at her with a knowing grin. 'You were positively drooling over those kids.'

She shrugged. 'Maybe I was. But you didn't do so badly either. Sally was absolutely smitten by you.'

Luke laughed. 'Trish says the actor's motto is never work with animals or children.'

The mention of Trish made Sophie stiffen. 'How is Trish?' she asked casually, glancing at Luke out of the corner of her eye.

'Fine, as far as I know. India has been seen again by their local vet and is seventy-five per cent better, but she won't be doing any competing in any shows this summer.'

Sophie digested the information. She hadn't realised Luke had seen Trish again since they had been at Long-haven.

'She must be disappointed,' Sophie answered flatly.

'I've no idea,' he shrugged. 'I couldn't speak to her for very long. I had a patient with me.'

Relief suddenly replaced dismay. So, it had been just a phone call. Sophie couldn't believe she could feel so bitter about Patricia De Vere, but she was such an objectionable woman.

'Let's do something different tonight,' she said on impulse. 'Let's go out for dinner, dance perhaps . . . maybe to the Moathouse?'

He lifted his broad shoulders on a sigh. 'Wish we could. I'm on call, remember?'

'Oh, yes, I'd forgotten.' She forced her gaze back on the road.

'Perhaps at the weekend,' he said gently.

'Yes, perhaps then.'

She kept her eyes on the road with studied concentration. The weekend would arrive, as she knew it would, with inevitable swiftness.

Her life, somehow, seemed as though it was held in suspension. The inevitability of his leaving the house and what would happen afterwards was cutting her in two. Luke was her other half; he fitted her.

But he did not love her.

★ ★ ★

In fact, when the weekend came Howard called around with Molly in the afternoon.

They brought their grandchildren with them, who were both Sally's and Simon's ages and who, with exuberance, played hide-and-seek with Steamer and Howard's Labrador, Goldie, all over the house and garden.

Sophie reflected wryly that some unseen hand was making a point about children. Perhaps if they wreaked havoc, she told herself, she would be put off for life, but instead they all decided to go to the river and walk the dogs.

Come the evening, Luke was called out to help John at a farm with a cow that had gone down and needed to be hoisted to its feet.

Luke returned at ten, looking worn out. They could only manage to find two farm hands to help shift the cow, which had chosen to collapse in the dairy entrance.

'Come here, you!' She enfolded him into her arms. He kissed her, his growth of beard scratching her face.

'Ouch,' she complained, pulling her face away.

'I'll shave,' he offered doubtfully. 'And shower.'

She shook her head, removing his damp shirt, and pushed him down on the sofa. Finding her oils, she rubbed the scented fragrance into his tired muscles, moving over the bones with a seductive, kneading stroke.

In ten minutes he was fast asleep.

★　★　★

The Sunday morning dawned with grey skies and Sophie turned over to the warm body beside her. At some unearthly hour during the night he had crawled into bed from his makeshift nest on the sofa downstairs. She hadn't disturbed him, just laid a blanket over his expended body and turned the side-lamp to low.

Vaguely, she had felt his breath on her shoulder, she remembered. Then they had fallen asleep again, in one another's arms.

Now she gazed into the sleepy blue eyes, fully opened, felt his heat burning across the bed as he drew her to him. 'Sorry about last night.'

She moved her head on the pillow, staring into the huge black pupils.

'Sophie, I've been thinking . . . '

She smiled wearily. 'You told me not to. Too much thinking is bad for you, you said.'

He pushed his fingers into her hair and opened his mouth to reply.

'Don't say it,' she whispered, unable to stand his pity or a piteous word.

'Are we separating because it's best for the practice or best for us?' he asked, despite her plea.

She paused, waiting for her heartbeat to slow. 'Does it matter which?'

He slipped his hands down the smooth skin of her neck, gently caressed her breast. 'You're right, let's stop talking,' he groaned. 'Do you mind my beard?'

'I don't mind anything this morning,'

she admitted truthfully, the familiar quickening of her body at his touch making her swallow hard.

He kissed her, made sweet, interminable love to her all morning, but there was already a distance between them. The heated intensity was edged with an unfamiliar uncertainty.

But in her heart she would always remember this morning and his perfect body and what it did to her. She would always remember his smile and its brilliance.

How she would manage at work, she didn't dare contemplate now. She must take each day individually.

Perhaps her mother was right. Perhaps this house was unkind to them. Who knew, but in a few weeks, when he had been away from her, the strength of her love would reunite them?

★　★　★

A thought she quickly dismissed the very next day as, while opening the mail in her office, she heard sobs from along the corridor.

Jane hurried in, her face red as she hesitated.

'What is it?' Sophie asked, frowning.

'More trouble for Luke, I think,' Jane said as she glanced over her shoulder. 'It's Amanda Drew. She won't talk to anyone, just Luke.'

'And Luke's in consultation.'

Jane nodded.

Sophie sighed. 'You'd better bring her in here.'

A few seconds later Amanda walked into her office with Jane giving her a little push.

'OK, Jane, thanks.' Sophie got up from her desk. 'Let Luke know, will you, before his next client?'

When the nurse had gone she pulled some tissues from a box and handed them to the sobbing girl.

'Th . . . thanks.' She dabbed at her eyes, her makeup running in rivulets down her cheeks.

'Coffee?' Sophie asked gently.

Amanda shook her head.

'Well, I think I'll have some.' Sophie sighed. How could she help the girl? she wondered. And if she couldn't, how many patients would she have to divert while Luke attended to her?

Feeling uncharitable, she made two coffees anyway and pushed a cup into Amanda's clenched hands.

'Come on, drink up,' she said cheerfully, kneeling down to peer into the girl's unhappy face. 'It's not the end of the world.'

'It m . . . might as well be,' Amanda choked as she gripped the cup with trembling fingers. 'I . . . I have to tell Luke. I . . . I'm three months pregnant.'

11

At that moment Luke came in.

Amanda propelled herself from the chair into his arms.

Sophie stared at the girl, transfixed by her heaving shoulders and Luke's face above.

'What in heaven's name — ?' he began as Amanda clung to him, sobbing.

'L . . . Luke, I'm p . . . pregnant,' she stammered, her fingers pulling at his shirt. 'Oh, God, Luke, what shall we do?'

Sophie blinked. There it was, in one, small sentence, the end of her world. Luke and Amanda Drew.

For once, he was speechless, his hands on Amanda's shoulders as he gazed disbelievingly into her face.

The silence seemed to go on forever, before he asked, 'Are you sure?'

Amanda nodded, tears streaming down her face.

Sophie forced herself to ask, 'Do you want to talk in here?'

Luke hesitated, staring down at the hysterical girl in his arms. Then he shook his head. 'No, I'll take her into my room. As for my clients — '

'I had better cancel all your morning's list,' she cut in stiffly. 'I'll see Howard and John.'

He nodded. 'Thanks.'

Without a word more he steered Amanda off and Sophie sat down, her legs seeming to have lost the power to stand as Jane reappeared, coming in to close the door quietly behind her.

Sophie looked up. 'Everyone heard, I suppose?'

Jane blushed. 'She made such a drama of it when she came in, didn't seem to be at all embarrassed, almost as if she wanted everyone to know that Luke — ' She clamped her mouth shut, closing her eyes.

Sophie understood full well what

Jane had been going to say. It meant that just about everyone knew that she and Luke had been having an affair. The fact that Amanda was pregnant and obviously wanted the world to know degraded every single moment she and Luke had spent together.

Three months pregnant. April. Just when Luke had first started with the practice, when he had bumped into Amanda at the Moathouse on Howard's and Molly's anniversary.

'See what you can do about Luke's clients,' she sighed distractedly. 'Either add them to John's or Howard's list or, if they don't want to see any vet but Luke, book them in for another morning.'

Jane nodded. 'Sophie, I'm so sorry. Is there anything I can do?'

'Not much.' She managed a smile. 'I'll cope, thanks.'

Jane hesitated, decided after a while not to prolong Sophie's embarrassment, quietly leaving the room and closing the door behind her.

Sophie gazed into space, hearing Amanda's words, seeing her tear-stained face. A feeling of numbness was creeping over her and she knew she should be thankful for it. Later would come the pain and humiliation, the terrible ache of discovery, veiled at the moment by the necessity to keep up appearances for the practice's sake.

What was it her mother had said? She could only go forward from here. It was true. There was no going back. Fate had made it so this morning in the cruellest of ways, the most heart-rending. But wasn't it better like this? She would never have got Luke out of her system. Now she had no choice. And nor did Luke.

★ ★ ★

Tempted to pack all his clothes in a suitcase like the proverbial spurned lover and fling it outside the front door, Sophie walked aimlessly around the house, her anger smouldering.

How could he have used her in such a way? Oh, he had never made her any promises and she knew his attitude full well regarding commitment. He had only wanted an affair with no strings attached and she knew it and had been forced to accept it. But all those nights of lovemaking, the passion and pleasure they had brought one another . . . did they really count for so little?

She had some pride left and she intended to keep it. Unable to remain at the practice a moment longer, she had left early. Luke had not returned and, though everyone had made the best of the situation, his absence on a busy Monday had been duly noted.

Howard and John had the decency not to ask her any questions. She knew they would have got enough information from Jane and Imelda, who had overheard every syllable no doubt.

She waited tensely in the drawing-room, her nerves stretched unmercifully, going the full gamut of reaction. Anger changed to disbelief and then back again to bitter humiliation.

He unlocked the front door at five and Steamer ran from his position at her feet to greet him.

Sophie sat where she was in the drawing-room. Pulling up her chin, she waited, listening to his tread through the house. When he came through the door, all her resolve came crashing down around her ears. In spite of everything, her love knew no bounds.

He came to stand beside her, broad shoulders hunched under the blue cotton shirt. 'Sophie, what can I say?' he muttered, his voice soft.

She looked up at him. 'What do you want to say?'

'A lot of things, but mostly that I'm sorry.'

Her eyes smarted, but she blinked back the tears. 'Well, you've said it. Now I think you'd better leave.'

His blue eyes suddenly lost their tiredness. 'What the hell do you mean?'

She stood up, clenching her hands. 'Exactly what I say. I don't want an argument or excuses, Luke, I'm too tired. Please, just leave.'

He stared at her incredulously. 'What on earth are you talking about? I know I made a mess of today, but that's no reason . . . '

'A mess?' Sophie repeated tremblingly, unable to believe what she was hearing. 'Surely that's a slight understatement?'

He frowned, staring hard at her, deep lines of anger forming around his mouth.

Her voice cracked as she managed to say, 'I've called a practice meeting for tomorrow morning. I think you owe John and Howard an explanation. They had the lion's share of the extra work to cope with. It would only be fair to explain . . . whatever it is you have to explain.'

He moved towards her angrily. 'I don't give a damn about a practice meeting. Listen to me, Sophie — '

She closed her eyes, still so stupidly susceptible to him. 'Luke, please, there's nothing you or I have left to say to one another. Don't make this even more difficult.'

'Sophie, you are making a big mistake,' he told her in a low voice.

'No, Luke, it's you who had made the mistake.'

He stared at her, frowning. 'Perhaps I have. I thought you would have been the first person to have given me the opportunity to explain.'

'Explain what? How can you explain away what happened today?' Her temper finally snapped, stretched beyond endurance. 'No, Luke, I'm not interested any more. I realise our relationship meant nothing to you. Perhaps it wasn't even a relationship in your eyes, just a fling!'

Pain flickered through his eyes as he stared at her.

Oh, God, she thought, don't let me weaken. 'A . . . as for the practice — '

'As for the practice,' he cut in slowly, his voice husky, 'you can keep it. You want perfection, Sophie, then you will have to find it with someone else. Because at eight-thirty tomorrow morning I'm telling Howard I'm finished here.' His blue eyes shimmered. 'As for my things, I'll come back and collect them some other time. When I don't have to undergo an inquisition into my private life — which has got damn all to do with anyone but myself.'

The next thing she heard was the slam of the front door. The whole house seemed to rock.

Had he genuinely supposed he could make love to her and pursue an affair with someone else at the same time? she wondered achingly.

She stumbled into the hall. His things were everywhere — a sweater, a coat, his scent in the air, his presence lingering in every room of the house. It felt like an indelible stain on her soul.

★   ★   ★

'I'm confused, to say the least,' Howard complained, scratching his head as he talked to Sophie in the office, the

310

following day. 'The man simply said, he'd given it a lot of thought, but in line with the three-month contract he feels he's just not cut out for the practice.'

Sophie nodded. 'Yes, I know. After what happened yesterday morning,' she lowered her gaze to the desk, unable to look Howard in the eye, 'in view of his domestic . . . problems . . . I suspected he might not wish to stay.'

Howard shrugged. 'I heard a lot of rubbish from Jane which, quite frankly, I don't blame Luke for entirely ignoring.'

Sophie sat forward. 'But it's true, Howard. I heard it myself.'

Howard shook his head. 'A young girl comes in hysterically sobbing all manner of nonsense and the whole of the staff are in uproar.' He frowned at her. 'You listened to his side of the story, of course?'

Sophie opened her eyes in surprise. 'What could he possibly say?'

Howard stared at her for a long while. Frowning, he lifted himself from the chair, digging his hands into his tweed jacket pockets. 'Perhaps you should ask him.' He walked slowly to the door, his shoulders drooping. 'I'd better get back. Will you see to advertising for a locum for the time being?'

Sophie nodded, her mouth dry. Her interview with Howard had not gone as she had expected. However, nothing Howard could say, or Luke, for that matter, could alter the fact that Amanda was pregnant with Luke's child.

★ ★ ★

Two weeks later to the day a new locum started.

The air was cool between Sophie and Luke, but, realising she could do nothing about the situation, she tried to ignore the bitterness in her heart eating away at her whenever she looked into his face.

The day Giles Grantham started a

hot July sun beamed its way across the top of her desk and came to rest on the golden lettering of her diary, fallen open at April.

Luke's name and the time of the interview was written at the top of the page.

Sophie closed the book and looked up to see Luke standing with Giles Grantham.

'I'm taking Giles with me on my calls,' he said in a distinctly over-polite tone.

Sophie nodded, smiling for Giles's sake. Hopefully he hadn't been initiated yet into staff gossip and wouldn't be for a while. Jane and Imelda were very discreet and hadn't mentioned the Amanda incident again. Still, she had more to think of than gossip at the moment and she rose from her desk, still with the smile plastered on her face.

'It's nice to have you with us, Giles. Welcome.'

The young red-haired man grinned.

'Nice to be here, Mrs Shaw.'

'Sophie, please,' she corrected gently, her eyes avoiding Luke's.

'I'll see you about last details,' Luke added in the same distant tone of voice.

Sophie nodded. 'When do you propose to leave?'

'Friday,' came the swift reply.

Four days to go. It was like an icy wind blowing in her face. She felt she was on an emotional seesaw as she watched the two men depart, going to her window, the one which overlooked the car park. How ridiculous to watch furtively like this.

Luke climbed into the driver's seat of the Jaguar and Giles into the passenger. The car purred by and she stepped back, catching sight of Luke's shadowed features below the sun visor.

Nothing could have prepared her for the loneliness she had felt since he had left the house. Two long, achingly empty weeks had passed and the house felt like a tomb. Without his laughter, his humour, his presence to

314

fill it, it seemed a shell.

Howard had mentioned that Luke's intention was to leave the district. Paradoxically, she willed the day to come when the torture would be over and then, in the next instant, dreaded it.

Trying her best to drag her thoughts back to work, she peeled herself from the window and sank back in her chair behind the desk. In front of her were the new work schedules, minus Luke's name. She blinked hard, trying to concentrate, the effort exhausting.

Then the internal phone rang and she picked it up, grateful for the distraction.

'Sophie,' Jane's voice faltered, 'a Mrs Cavanagh to see you. Shall I send her in?'

'Mrs Cavanagh? Do I know her? Is she a client?'

'It's a personal matter, apparently.'

Sophie hesitated, saying the name over again to herself. Unable to bring a face to mind, she told Jane to go ahead and send her in.

Seconds later a slim woman in her early thirties appeared. She had long straight fair hair clipped up on either side of her head with combs, revealing an attractive, intelligent face, her lips turned up in a hesitant smile.

Sophie felt she should recognise her; there was something vaguely familiar, but she couldn't decide what.

She held out her hand and the woman grasped it.

'I feel I should know you,' Sophie apologised hesitantly. She gestured to the chair beside the desk, admiring the graceful movements, the gentle composure of the woman's face. And something else . . .

'I thought you might recognise my voice,' her guest said softly. 'I recognised yours immediately from our brief telephone conversations.' At Sophie's deepening frown, she added, 'I'm Louise Cavanagh, Luke's sister.'

Sophie's smile faltered as she took a breath. Those piercing blue eyes — of course! So much like Luke's. The fair hair and petite build had distracted her from the stunning similarity.

Louise Cavanagh clasped her hands tightly in her lap. 'Sophie, I'm sorry to barge in like this, but I'm returning to Cambridge this evening because of Pip.'

Sophie asked hesitantly, 'How is she?'

'Much better, thanks. Martin is with her. She's out of hospital — I expect Luke told you.'

Sophie dropped her gaze. She liked this woman instinctively. But to discuss Luke was hurtful and she had no intention of doing so. She shook her head, lifting her eyes. 'You must be very relieved.'

Louise nodded. 'You don't realise how much a child means until you think you might lose them.' Her words were quietly delivered, but Sophie recognised the worry lines and tinge of bluish skin which indicated long hours of anxiety.

'And how can I help?' she asked, unwilling to prolong the conversation more than necessary if Louise was just biding time waiting for her brother to return from his calls.

'It's about Luke — '

Sophie stiffened, her face paling.

'Please hear me out?' Louise Cavanagh sat on the edge of the seat, her fingers grasping the desk. 'Your receptionist explained that Luke would not be back just yet.' She looked under her lashes. 'He would be furious if he knew I was talking to you like this, but he's a man with a great deal of pride, which I'm afraid may be the cause of a deep misunderstanding between you.'

Sophie frowned. 'But how do you know all this?'

Louise paused. 'We speak frequently on the phone. Last time he told me he had decided to leave the practice.'

Sophie nodded, her eyes wary.

'Though he hasn't explained fully, I gather he has had trouble with Patricia De Vere and her sister?'

Sophie stared at her blankly. 'I'm sorry?'

'Amanda Drew?' Louise prompted. 'De Vere is Patricia's stage name. Their maiden name is Drew.' Louise sighed, looking directly at Sophie with her brother's blue eyes. 'Luke met Patricia and Amanda at a Paris horse sale five years ago. Amanda was just fourteen and had been expelled from boarding-school for experimenting with drugs. Patricia was hoping a trip to Europe might help her. You see, Amanda's mother died after her birth and their father remarried a woman neither of them liked. Patricia tried to take an interest in her sister, but, between her acting career and numerous husbands, the girl became uncontrollable.'

Louise frowned as she added quietly, 'Luke's brief affair with Patricia when she was between husbands was over in a matter of months, but by then Amanda idolised him. He was patient and sympathetic and felt desperately sorry for the child. His own years in boarding-school had been equally unhappy. But my brother took on too much. Patricia and Amanda seemed to have unending problems. Martin and I tried to warn him . . . but he always felt responsible for the girl.'

'But I thought — '

'You thought Luke was involved romantically?' She gave a mirthless laugh. 'Oh, no. He's just a very softhearted guy who couldn't say no to Patricia's constant appeals for support and Amanda's little outbursts.'

'But why didn't he explain this to me?' Sophie asked in bewilderment. 'I would have understood.'

Louise arched her eyebrows. 'I suppose because he thought it was unfair to involve you. Martin and I warned him his silence might rebound and of course it did. Amanda got pregnant by her latest boyfriend and was terrified of telling Patricia. I believe you got the brunt of it that day.'

Amanda's words flew through Sophie's brain. If what Louise had to say was true, she had completely misread the situation.

'Luke is extremely fond of you,' Louise persisted gently. 'I just couldn't bear to watch him walk away from someone he thought so much of because of the Drews — and his stupid pride.'

Sophie met her gaze. 'It's too late,' she sighed helplessly.

Louise shook her head. 'I learnt a great deal from Pip's accident. When she was in a coma we sat by her and simply prayed. I promised that when she woke I would never again let a day pass without telling her I loved her.' She gazed across the desk with gentle blue eyes. 'It's never too late, Sophie.'

★   ★   ★

The chestnuts around the house were in full bloom as Sophie drove up in her Volvo estate, scanning the windows for a sign of life. Howard had told her Luke had come here to close up and return the keys to the estate agents. Though Luke had not returned to stay at the house after their argument, preferring to return to the Cranthorpe Arms, there were, apparently, still a few small items left to be collected.

Sophie pulled on the brake, her heart thumping in her chest. The place looked deserted. Was she too late? And anyway, what would she say?

What was it Luke had accused her of? Indulging in large amounts of guilt. Well, it had been true. She had languished in guilt since Michael had died, but now it was different.

Oh, so different.

As she hurried towards the front door the gravel crunched under her feet, her heels making her stumble, her pencil-slim skirt over her slender legs restricting her movement. Brushing back untidy wisps of blonde hair, she pushed her hand hard on the bell.

Undecided as to whether it was working, she ran to one of the big bay windows and peered in, shielding the evening sunlight from her face with her hand.

No sign of life.

The empty room was exactly as she remembered it and her heart lurched. Luke had been so full of plans, so eager to discuss them with her.

She stepped back. If he was here the Jaguar would have been parked outside. She gave a little sigh. How silly; she had just had false hope.

It was no use. The place was deserted.

'Sophie?'

She spun around, her brown eyes widening at the tall figure standing there.

Luke stared at her, his dark head tilted to one side. A pain went through her that left her breathless. How much she loved him. Loved every inch of his long, lean body. Dressed as he was in thigh-hugging jeans and dark blue T-shirt, his presence came over in strong, throat-tightening waves.

'I . . . I couldn't see the Jag,' she mumbled stupidly. She couldn't say what was in her heart; her pride still wouldn't let her do that.

'It's parked at the back.' He paused. 'Is there something wrong?' He frowned, the blue eyes washing over her, making her tremble inside.

She nodded. For a moment she was tempted to fling herself into his arms and risk rejection, but she held back.

'The practice?' He took a step towards her, concern etched in his face.

'No. It's . . . me, Luke. I've been so horribly wrong. I . . . I . . . said all those dreadful things. I wouldn't listen — '

He stiffened, comprehension in his expression. 'Yes,' he agreed coldly. 'You were wrong, Sophie.'

She hung her head, staring at her white-knuckled fingers. 'Louise came today,' she confessed. 'She told me everything.'

Making her jump, he was suddenly standing in front of her, his face furious. 'Louise?'

She nodded, staring up at him. 'Please don't blame her, Luke. She made me understand. I was so . . .

jealous, so hurt. I was blinded, because . . . I loved you so much. Louise could understand that. I hoped, at least if you couldn't find it in your heart to forgive me — '

'Forgive you!' The hard lines of anger suddenly disappeared, his taut body softening as he reached out and pulled her into his arms. 'Sophie, you'll never know how much I've missed you.'

'Oh, Luke!' Her voice was a broken whisper as she buried her head in his chest, repressing the tears that were so near to falling, a tremor of need going through her body.

'Shh, it's all right,' he whispered gently, holding her so tightly that she could almost hear the muscles in his body stretch and contract beneath the strong brown skin. Her fingers ran over the firmness of his arms and up into his hair. Her breath came in soft, short gasps as he leaned down to cover her mouth with his own.

She kissed him back with all the pain and frustration of the last two weeks, the ache inside her exploding until it began to dissolve as her lips melted to his, the heat of their bodies burning them together in long-held-back need.

'Oh, God, Sophie, it's been such a mess,' he whispered, planting tiny kisses all over her face.

Her fevered lips opened quiveringly. 'Luke, I thought Amanda's child was yours. I was so wrong. I didn't understand. Can you ever forgive me?'

He took her hot face between his hands. 'I should have told you about Amanda and Patricia. I persuaded myself it wasn't necessary. Why should I tell you? I asked myself. Our relationship was separate . . . we seemed to be living in our own little world. But every so often something cropped up. Louise said it wasn't fair. That if I thought anything of you I should explain.' He pulled her lips to his mouth. 'But I was scared. Scared of admitting I thought enough of you to let you into my life.'

She felt the beat of his heart beneath her own, lifting her eyes to him solemnly. 'What is it that frightens you? Is it being cared for . . . loved too much?'

He shook his head, the blue eyes going sadly over her anguished face. 'No, that I might lose something I loved. If I didn't feel love in the first place, there would be no risk. But when we almost lost Pip I realised it was impossible to live life without loving — or losing. When I came home to you I tried to convince myself it wasn't true, that I hadn't fallen in love with you . . . but it was useless. I loved you more than ever.'

She hugged him, her eyes filling with tears. How long had she waited to hear those words? The terrible thing was, she didn't deserve to hear them after she had doubted him.

'Luke, you don't have to say it. I want you, under any terms — '

He put his hand firmly over her mouth. 'We are starting again, Sophie, right from this moment. I want it to be right this time.'

When he slid it away she was smiling. 'It's crazy. What are we going to do? What about the practice — ?'

'The practice can take care of itself. We've another pair of hands now — Giles. He's good. We'll keep him.'

She gasped. 'You make it sound simple.'

'It is simple, believe me.' He stared unwaveringly into her eyes. 'I took Amanda back to her sister and told them they had to sort out their own lives. Not that it should be too difficult. The father of the child is one of Trish's young house guests, so they all ought to be able to keep an eye on one another.'

Sophie burst into laughter. 'I'm sorry, I can't help feeling . . . so wonderful!' Then a hard lump formed in her throat as she thought of how she had nearly lost him.

He tipped up her chin, his blue eyes questioning. 'Sophie, are you sure about us?'

A sob escaped her lips. She had never been more sure of anything in her life.

'Your life with me will be very different to the one you led with Michael,' he threatened.

'My life . . . with you?'

'For instance, we shall need some more help on the administrative side very soon.'

Her smile faded. 'But Lucy — '

He grinned. 'I'm not talking about Lucy.'

'Then . . . ?'

'After we are married — '

'M . . . married!'

'You'll have precious little time to worry about the books. I'd say about nine months, in all.'

'Nine months . . . '

'Nine months, hopefully, to this very day,' he growled as he swept her off her feet and pulled her into his chest, lunging out with his foot to give the front door a firm push.

To her amazement it swung open. 'I'm carrying you over the threshold a little early, Mrs Jordon . . . but I don't think we'll quibble over details, do you?'

'Oh, Luke, I love you,' she breathed in answer, her heart so full that it felt it was about to burst.

'And I love you,' he whispered as they began to ascend the stairs.

THE END